AF254523

THE FIREFIGHTER'S FIANCÉ

CHRISTIAN CONTEMPORARY ROMANCE

FULLER FAMILY IN BRUSH CREEK ROMANCE

BOOK TWO

LIZ ISAACSON

Copyright © 2020 by Elana Johnson, writing as Liz Isaacson

All rights reserved.

No part of this book may be reproduced in any form or by any electronic or mechanical means, including information storage and retrieval systems, without written permission from the author, except for the use of brief quotations in a book review.

ISBN-13: 978-1638760887

"Knowing this, that the trying of your faith worketh patience.

But let patience have her perfect work, that ye may be perfect and entire, wanting nothing."

James 1:3-4

CHAPTER 1

Cora Wesley tipped her head back, the bottom of her ponytail brushing down her back as she laughed. The atmosphere in the karaoke bar vibrated with energy, with sound waves from the stage, with chatter and laughter and friendship.

She quieted, realizing she was the only woman at the table of firefighters. She'd been in Brush Creek for a year and had gotten used to the nearly female-free department, but she knew she sometimes stuck out like that one Christmas light that kept blinking when it was supposed to stay steady.

She picked up her strawberry lemonade and licked the sugary rim while the firefighter currently telling jokes started in on another one. A pause of silence in the music behind her alerted her to the change in singers, and the next song began. A horrible, nasally voice started on the lyrics, causing her to twist to see what poor soul had decided to take the mic and try to sing an Adele song—clearly out of her vocal range.

Not that Cora was a good singer by any stretch of the imagination. But she knew her limits and wouldn't embarrass herself on purpose. The redhead on stage glanced around nervously, her eyes landing on a table of women a couple over from Cora and her squad of bulky firefighters. All the women had been eyeing their table the entire evening, and while none of her firemen buddies had made a move, they'd all noticed.

The amount of flexing and loud laughter testified of that. Cora couldn't help joining in. She liked her friends at Station House Two, and if she didn't come out on Friday nights with them, she'd be excluded in their camaraderie by more than her gender.

Plus, she liked going out with them. There were only so many hours in a day that she could run and lift weights. She drained the last of her lemonade, vowing not to order another. She wasn't big by any stretch of the imagination, but she needed to meet certain physical standards to apply for the interagency hotshot crews. She wanted the Great Basin crew, so she could stay in Utah, Idaho, and Nevada. But Cora would take any crew that would take her.

So with a determination to put in another fifty pushups after she returned to her solitary, quite apartment that night, she tuned back in to Jorge's joke about a duck and why he couldn't cross the road.

As the other men broke into another round of

raucous laughter, her phone blinked and vibrated the table in front of her. She swiped it into her lap to read her sister's text. Helene was already married and settled in Vernal, where Cora's parents lived. Where she'd been raised.

Mom wants to know if you're coming to the family anniversary party.

Cora's stomach twisted and her mouth felt sour—and not because of the lemonade she'd drunk. The family anniversary party was a celebration of the day the Wesley family had begun—the day her parents had gotten married forty years ago.

She started thumbing out a response when Helene added *It's a big one. Forty years.*

Cora erased her rejection to her older sister. She couldn't miss the forty-year anniversary. Thirty-nine, sure. Forty-one, definitely. But not this one.

She sighed, her mind far from the party atmosphere now. The waitress approached their table, and her friends ordered more sodas, but Cora waved her hand. Someone asked her something, but her thoughts lingered on what family functions used to be like for her. They were so much easier when she had someone to attend them with.

"Do you want to add your name to the list?" Charlie, the man seated next to her, asked.

"Yeah, sure," she said distractedly, an idea churning in her head now. If she could take someone to the family anniversary party, things would be easier for everyone. No one knew what to say to her now, without Brandt on her arm. She glanced at the six men she spent most of her life with. Maybe one of them....

She banished the thought before it could truly take root. Her ex, Brandt, had been a firefighter, and she wasn't interested in getting involved with another one. They were great friends. Great boyfriends. Not great husbands, at least in her experience.

She knew she was being totally unfair. There were several married firefighters and their wives seemed happy enough. *It was just a bad match*, she told herself, signaling for another lemonade despite her promise to herself.

Well? Are you coming?

Helene wouldn't be put off, and if Cora didn't answer her, she'd call. So Cora picked up her phone and said, *Yes, I'll be there.*

Bringing anyone?

At that moment, Charlie plucked her phone from her hand. "You're missing out," he said, placing it face-down on the table on his left, out of her reach.

"It's my sister," she said, panic rearing in her chest now.

"Kent asked what song you're singing." Charlie nodded to the man sitting next to Cora on her other side.

Confusion needled her. "Singing?" She scoffed. "I'm not singing." Sure, she'd come to the karaoke bar, but she never sang.

"You told Charlie to tell Sissy to put you on the list,"

Kent said. "I thought it was weird." He nodded toward the phone. "Let me see that."

Cora made a lunge for her device as Charlie passed it over to him, both of them chuckling. She'd learned in the first day at the Brush Creek Fire Department not to keep anything sensitive on her phone. They got passed around like sticks of gum, and she sometimes texted her mates from someone else's phone.

"It's nothing," she said.

"Family anniversary party," Kent read, his dark eyes squinting in concentration. A whistle followed. "Wow, forty years." He handed the phone back to her. "Are you going with anyone?"

No one in Brush Creek knew she'd been married before, and she wanted to keep it that way. She'd dated at least a dozen men in the year she'd been in town. Dated wasn't really the right word. She went to dinner with a guy and then didn't call him back. Or hung out with a man for a couple of weeks before settling into friend territory.

She'd met a few men that stirred her interest, but her goal of landing on a hotshot crew always kept her focus away from starting something serious. She simply wasn't interested in serious.

"I don't know." Cora sighed out her answer. She looked at Kent and then Charlie, wondering if she could ask one of them to go with her. Kent probably would. He'd been one she'd eaten burgers with and then brushed off.

Kent flipped her ponytail like an annoying older brother. "Still no boyfriend, then?"

Cora snorted, all the answer that question required.

The conversation at the table quieted, and Cora glanced around, wondering if her disgust at Kent's question had really been that loud.

"Go on, then," Jorge said, folding his giant arms and making his biceps bulge. It was a miracle the women a couple of tables over didn't faint at the sight.

"Go on where?" Cora asked, reaching for her refilled glass of lemonade.

"They just called your name." He nodded toward the stage, and Cora whipped her attention behind her so fast her neck sent a shock of pain down her spine.

Kent nudged her out of her seat and Charlie pushed her toward the steps amidst her protests. Along the way, she passed a table of men, all of them with sandy hair and light eyes. They smiled at her in what she was sure was meant to be encouragement.

She knew who they were; everyone knew the Fullers. But she didn't know any of the men by name, only reputation, and when one nodded at her, his grin fading to the natural strong set of his jaw, she paused.

All noise fell away, leaving just a silent conduit from her to this handsome Fuller man seated furthest from her.

Somehow, her feet took her up the steps to the stage, and it seemed like everyone in the bar had suddenly run out of things to say to one another. With sixty pairs of eyes on her, she gripped the mic and pointed to the song she wanted to sing.

The music started, a slow ballad of a childhood song she'd grown up belting out with her brother and sister. She closed her eyes just before starting on the first line, really losing herself to the moment and hoping with everything in her that she didn't make a complete fool of herself.

"Lying in my bed, I hear the clock tick and think of you."

She opened her eyes, her gaze locking onto the man watching her intently now. One of his brothers elbowed him, but he didn't look away from her.

Cora didn't need to look at the screen to keep singing. She belted out the chorus with accuracy, putting on a good show as she became aware of her firefighter crew yelping and whooping their encouragement.

But she absolutely couldn't look away from the mystery man who'd captured her attention in a single moment of time.

He got up and went over to the table where she'd been sitting with her back to him, leaning down to say something to Charlie. Kent joined the conversation, and Cora's blood boiled because no doubt they were talking about her.

"Time after time," she sang into the mic. "Time after time." One last big breath, and she ended with another, "Time after time," in the best breathy Cyndi Lauper voice she could muster. The 80s music faded, leaving only her, alone on the stage in her tight black jeans and flowing black tank top, her hand dropping to her side as if the mic were too heavy to hold up for another moment.

She handed it to Sissy and stumbled toward the steps, at the bottom of which Kent and Charlie were now clapping. Before she'd even gotten both feet on solid ground, Kent pushed her toward the man who'd singlehandedly gotten her pulse racing and said, "Here's your next date, Cora."

She fumbled into him, her hands landing solidly on his chest. His very solid, wide chest.

Cora swallowed, righted herself, and glared at Kent. "I'm not looking for a date."

"Sure you are," Charlie said. "To your parent's party."

Humiliation crept up Cora's back and down her arms. "You guys—no." She met the Fuller man's eyes and nearly drowned in the beautiful depths of them. "No offense," she managed to squeak out.

My, he was handsome. Tall. With loads of sandy hair that would surely glide right through her fingers like silk. And those hazel eyes that looked dark as chocolate in this dim bar lighting.

"I'm Brennan Fuller," he said, extending his hand toward her to shake. "I don't think we've met."

That same floaty feeling that had happened the first time they'd looked at one another happened again.

Kent's voice faded. Charlie's body behind her, trapping her close to Brennan, disappeared.

There was just this Brennan Fuller man wearing half a coy smile, and Cora. The two of them breathed in and out together, and Cora found herself saying, "I'm Cora Wesley. How do you feel about stuffy anniversary parties with dozens of married people?"

CHAPTER 2

Brennan Fuller didn't meet many angels. None, in fact. But the bronze-skinned woman with well-defined muscles in her upper arms seemed to have a golden glow about her. Her nearly black hair wisped out of its high ponytail, which extended halfway down her back. Her eyes should've been darker than they were, but shone with a light brown shade that made her even more exotic.

Self-consciousness ripped through him. She'd surely forget all about him by morning, the way most women did. Most everyone, in fact. Brennan had a most forgettable face, something he'd been reminded of every day of his life growing up. Being the fourth of four boys could do that to a person, and sometimes his mother went through all her other son's names before landing on the right one for him.

"Stuffy anniversary parties with dozens of married

people are my specialty," he said. Brennan would've done almost anything to get to know who this beauty was. Just standing up and approaching the firemen table had proven that. He hadn't noticed her sitting there before, as her back had been toward him. But he'd felt something cascade through him as she'd walked by, her eyes meeting his and hooking on tight.

That ice water feeling in his blood had intensified when she'd started singing, and when his oldest brother had nudged him and told him to stop staring, Brennan had made a snap decision.

"Great." She held out her hand, but he had no idea what she wanted and lifted his eyes back to her face.

"What?"

"I'll put my number in your phone." She lifted her chin as if daring him to offer a different solution. Brennan could think of many, only one of which was to link his arm with hers and take her somewhere quieter so they could talk. So he could stare at her and bask in that angelic glow that had him tongue-tied and jittery.

"Give her your phone, man," Kent Hammer said, a man that Brennan had grown up with in Brush Creek.

Brennan sprang into action, withdrawing his phone from his pocket and placing it in Cora's delicate hand.

Kent asked him something about the landscaping Brennan did, but the words swirled around inside his head, not making any sense. Cora's long fingers tapped and swiped on his phone, and then those mesmerizing eyes landed on him again as she flipped it over and extended it toward him.

"There you go."

He took it, the plastic case warm from her touch, a sense of wonder flowing through him like warm honey.

"Call me," she said just before twisting sharply so that her hair jumped. She strode away, Kent and Charlie in her wake, none of them looking back. Somehow, Brennan managed to stumble back to the table where his brothers sat, all three of them with gigantic smiles on their faces.

"So, what's her name?" Milt asked just as the waiter set down another basket of cheese-topped French fries.

"Cora." Brennan straightened his collar and didn't meet any of his brother's eyes.

"Oh, *Cora*," Patrick sighed out before laughing.

"I didn't say it like that."

"Totally did, bro," Kyler said, the other unmarried Fuller man. Milt and Pat had both been married for a couple of years, and Pat's wife had just delivered their first child six months ago.

"*Coraaaah*," Milt sighed, holding onto the last vowel as if he were British.

Brennan couldn't help the quick laugh that passed his lips. "Shut up, you guys." He ducked his head and looked over to her table. She sat up straight and tall while all the other men at the table slouched a bit. She totally didn't fit with all the muscled firefighters, but at the same time, she really did.

Everything about her intrigued him, and he wanted to rush out and call her right now. Instead, he endured another hour of bad karaoke and the ribbing of his brothers before returning to his one-bedroom house nestled in a quiet cul-de-sac, where he found his lazy basset hound sound asleep on his bed.

He collapsed onto the comforter, jostling Sybil to wakefulness and petting her as he said, "I met the most amazing woman tonight, Syb."

The basset hound didn't seem to care at all about Cora, her snores steadying despite Brennan's details of the few minutes he'd shared with Cora in the karaoke bar.

His phone rang, and he swiped it on after barely glancing at it. It would be his grandpa Daryl, probably needing help with something like his coffee maker not working. The last time he'd called about an appliance, it hadn't worked because it wasn't plugged in. Neither his grandfather nor his grandmother had even checked that.

"Hey, Gramps," he said, sitting up. "What's up?"

"Can't find Pops," he said, his voice old and ragged.

"Did you check under the deck by the shed?" Brennan asked. "He likes to hide there in the summer."

It had been hot the past few days, the first sign that summer had truly arrived in Brush Creek. The first week of June, rain had flirted with the town relentlessly, keeping things cool in the morning and the afternoon. But that had dried up, and the wind had started, and it really felt like summer now.

"Grams checked there. He's gone."

The little schnauzer was about as old as his owners and if he got out of the backyard, he couldn't find his way back.

"When did you let him out?"

"A few hours ago. Then we started a movie, and I forgot about him."

Brennan sighed, though he wasn't really too upset. "I'll be right over, Gramps. Maybe get out some cheese and sit on the front steps. Maybe he'll come back when he smells the treat."

He hung up and shoved his phone in his back pocket before looking back at Sybil. "I'm headed over to find Pops. Want to come?"

Sybil didn't even open her eyes, which Brennan took for a *no, thank you, I'm snoozing right now*. He chuckled and headed out to his truck. The sun had gone down an hour ago, leaving the temperatures to cool a bit.

He arrived at his paternal grandparent's house to find Gramps sitting on the front steps, whistling for Pops and waving around a bit of cheese to no avail.

"Nothing?" Brennan asked, though he hadn't really thought his suggested method would bring back the little dog.

"I can hear 'im barking," Gramps said. "But he doesn't come."

Brennan cocked his head to listen. "Whistle him again."

Gramps's weathered whistle lifted into the night air,

and sure enough Pops's equally hoarse bark sounded... somewhere.

Brennan twisted back to the house. "Gramps, he's inside." He got up and helped his grandpa stand. He held the screen door open while Gramps stepped inside, the barking becoming a bit louder.

"Grams?" he called.

"Oh, she went to bed," Gramps said, shuffling forward. "I think she's secretly hoping Pops will wander off and that'll be the end of him." He continued to mutter as he went into the kitchen.

Brennan headed downstairs to the basement, where his grandparents didn't go anymore in their advanced age. As a boy, Brennan had loved coming to sleep over at his grandparent's house. They knew his name. They remembered his favorite foods, and asked him about his science classes. Gramps had never missed a science decathalon competition, and Brennan had grown up believing that while he was constantly overshadowed in his core family, he was Gramps and Grams's favorite grandchild.

"Pops!" he called, stepping onto carpet at the bottom of the stairs that hadn't experienced a footprint in a while. The dog yapped and scratching came from behind the door to Brennan's right. He used to sneak down here in the summer, right into this storage room, where Grams kept popsicles in stock.

He pushed open the door and almost got plowed over by Pops. "What're you doin' down here?" He scooped the schnauzer into his arms. The fifteen-pound dog quivered, but Brennan went into the storage room and opened the freezer.

Several cartons of ice cream sat there, as well as three bags of popsicles. A grin popped onto his face, his plans to stop by every day for a treat blooming fully in his mind.

But he'd eaten enough at the karaoke bar to put a small pony out of commission for a while, so he simply closed the freezer, closed the door behind him, and took Pops upstairs.

"Here he is." He handed the dog to Gramps, who fed him the bite of cheese as he reprimanded him for wandering off.

Brennan exhaled as he sat at the bar. "So, Gramps, I met a woman today."

Gramps looked at him, his eyes bright and blue and boring right into Brennan. "Oh? I thought you said Brush Creek was a...what did you say?" He pretended to think and Brennan simply waited, his lips twitching the slightest bit.

"Oh, I remember. A barren wasteland when it came to women."

"It is. I don't want to go out with someone I grew up with." He was way past that stage. Most people who'd grown up together in Brush Creek had already gotten together. He wasn't suddenly going to be interested in Mindy Lee just because they were both still single.

"So who is she?"

"Her name's Cora. She's a firefighter. Been in town about a year."

"And you're just now meetin' her?"

"Yep. At the karaoke bar." Brennan spent most of his time with mowers and blowers, so yeah, he'd missed her arrival in town. In the fifteen seconds he'd had to ask Kent about her, he'd learned she'd been in town for a year and was interested in anyone who wasn't a fellow firefighter.

He fit the bill, and he was sure his obsessive staring had been enough to show his interest in her.

"I don't like the karaoke bar," Gramps said, his frown creating deep lines in his wrinkled face.

Brennan chuckled. "I know, Gramps. I know."

His phone vibrated and then sounded, and he pulled it out to look at it. "Unknown." He frowned, wondering if he'd look like Gramps in fifty years. He glanced up to find the old man watching him. "Should I answer it?"

"Could be Cora," Gramps said, but Brennan shook his head.

"It won't be Cora." She wasn't the type to give out her number and then call him. She'd make him come to her. Brennan made a quick decision and swiped open the call. "Hello?"

"Is this Brennan Fuller?" a woman asked. Music played in the background, almost like she was still at the karaoke bar.

"Cora?"

"Yeah." She giggled, an intoxicating sound that sent

Brennan's pulse into a tailspin. "I was wondering if you could get together sooner rather than later. We probably need to go over a few things if you're to be my boyfriend next weekend."

Brennan shot to his feet. "Boyfriend?" He wished his voice wasn't quite so high and squeaky. Turning away from Gramps's curious gaze, he hissed, "No one said anything about me being your boyfriend."

CHAPTER 3

"Why do you think I'm calling?" Cora asked, pacing away from the karaoke bar. For the first time since she'd moved to Brush Creek, she wanted to go back inside. But the texts with Helene had intensified, and then Charlie had taken her phone and sent a few messages without her consent.

Before she knew it, Helene thought the man she was bringing to the family anniversary party was her boyfriend. A very serious boyfriend. A boyfriend who had mentioned diamonds.

Cora pressed her eyes closed and wished with everything in her that she hadn't let her stupid firemen friends take over her phone. But she was in too deep now, and Kent had given her Brennan's number.

Brennan was so silent for so long, she wasn't sure if he was still on the call. "Well?" she asked. "What's your schedule like tomorrow?"

"Uh, my sister hasn't texted me yet. But I'll probably be at the rec center."

"You get your schedule from your sister?"

"Yeah, my family runs a handyman business. We do housecleaning, landscaping, painting, whatever you need. It's called A Jack of All Trades, and Wren manages the schedule for all of us." He cleared his throat. "Anyway, I'm usually free in the evenings."

Cora couldn't wait until evening. She had to prep this man she barely knew to meet her very inquisitive mother and sister, and she only had seven days to do it. Seven days. Panic clogged her throat. She might as well give up now. There was no way she could spend enough time with Brennan to make her family believe she'd been dating him long enough to be talking marriage.

The idea was laughable anyway, something she'd very sternly pointed out to Charlie. He'd laughed and said, "Oh, come on, Cora. You'll settle down eventually, won't you?"

She hadn't answered, instead, grabbing her phone and stalking out to the parking lot to make this call.

No, she didn't want to settle down. Brush Creek wasn't a permanent stop for her. It was an outlying town in a huge fire zone. It was a place she could get the experience she needed to put on her hotshot application. Though she wasn't particularly religious, she'd found herself praying for big wildfires in the wilderness surrounding Brush Creek, just so she could have some experience beyond a small ditch fire or a backyard barbeque gone awry.

"What about lunch?" she asked, opening her eyes and looking up to the stars. "I could just hang out with you while you work. I can mow a lawn or move dirt or whatever you're doing."

"Oh." The surprise in his tone wasn't hard to find. "I—I—"

"Maybe you can text me where you'll be, and when, and we can...talk." Her stomach coiled like a snake ready to strike. She wanted to believe she could get by at the party by disclosing to Brennan her favorite foods and colors, but she knew she'd have to tell him more than that.

Her throat felt like someone had poured acid down it. She'd have to tell him about Brandt.

"Uh, yeah, okay," Brennan said. "I'll text you."

"Great." Cora took a deep breath. "Things have gotten...a little out of hand with my family. It's just one party. Next Saturday. It'll probably take your whole day." If he was working tomorrow, maybe he wouldn't be able to come next weekend.

"I can get it off," he assured her. "I can do one party."

"I'll give you all the details tomorrow," she said. "I'm sorry."

"Don't be sorry," he said. "I was willing to go with you before, and that hasn't changed."

Cora nodded and said, "Great, see you tomorrow," before hanging up as quickly as possible. She didn't want to blurt out that they'd have to hold hands and possibly kiss at the party. He probably wouldn't want to come then.

She sighed and turned back to the entrance to the karaoke bar. *Although....* She relived the moment they'd looked at each other, and she couldn't believe that tether had only been present for her. He'd felt something too. Something strong enough to get up while she was singing and go talk to his old pal Kent.

Cora had said she'd be right back, but she headed for her bike instead. No text needed. Kent and Charlie had done enough for one night anyway. Maybe it would do them some good to think they'd caused her enough distress to run her off.

She swung her leg over her motorcycle and stuck the key in the ignition. Summer provided such freedom for Cora, and she fastened the strap of her helmet under her chin and set the bike north up the hills toward the strawberry fields instead of south toward her apartment down by the high school.

The cool darkness swept past her, pulling at her ponytail and releasing all of her pent-up anxiety. She'd moved to Brush Creek the weekend following the family anniversary last year, and she'd only been back to Vernal a few times over the past twelve months. Enough to show her family she still loved them. But not often enough to cause her mental distress.

The awkwardness she could expect to feel with her happily married sister and her equally blissful older brother crept upon her again. She simply didn't fit now that she was divorced and fully focused on getting a coveted and respected spot on an interagency hotshot crew.

There were only twenty spots per crew, and Cora desperately wanted one. She'd put in an application two years ago—the last time the open applications were being taken—and she'd been passed over time and time again. She'd relocate if she had to. Heck, she'd do *anything* if it meant she could get a spot on a hotshot crew.

She tipped her head back, increasing her speed until the headlamp on her motorcycle could barely show her what was coming before it came. With the speed, and the cold air, and sheer thrill of darkness surrounding her, her mind finally quieted.

By the time she returned to her apartment, she was ready to focus on her next problem: Brennan Fuller. As she bent to pick up her two American shorthair cats, Queenie and Cornelius, she wondered if they'd even be compatible enough to make it through a five-hour party.

Pippa, her great dane, bellowed a bark at her. "I know," she said. "I'm in real trouble." After all, *she* could barely make it through a five-hour party, and it was her own family. No way Brennan could survive that.

She filled food bowls and refreshed water, ignoring the sloppy way Pippa lapped like it was her first time drinking, and retreated to her bedroom. Her mind revolved through conversation topics for tomorrow, with facts she'd need to know about him for when her mom and sister pulled him away from her and began questioning her mercilessly.

A moan pulled through her throat, and she laid awake for a long time, wondering what she'd gotten herself into.

———

CORA WOKE to three texts from Brennan. He was indeed going to be at the recreation center for most of the day, weeding flower beds, trimming bushes, and barking "everything that isn't grass."

Cora didn't bother showering. Wasn't worth her time or effort if she was going to be spending the day outside with shears and wheelbarrows.

And a handsome man.

Fine, Brennan was pretty fine to look at. He'd seemed nice enough, and Kent had had nothing but good things to say about him. Apparently they'd grown up in Brush Creek together.

Cora arrived at the rec center at eight o'clock sharp, wondering which truck in this cowboy town belonged to Brennan. Doing landscaping and yard work as he did, he'd surely own a truck. She eyed a huge silver thing with wheels almost as tall as her as she crossed the lot toward the main entrance. Didn't seem like a truck Brennan would own, but how would she know?

She bypassed the front doors, spotting four bags of bark lying in the grass near some shrubs. Definitely on the right track to finding the man whose life she needed to memorize as quickly as possible.

Rounding the corner, she ran smack dab into something solid and covered with denim and gray cotton.

"Oof," Brennan said, catching her around the waist before she could rebound off his body.

"Sorry." She hastily backed up, smoothing down her own simple T-shirt. She couldn't help scanning him. With the brown leather work boots and the long, jean-clad legs, and that T-shirt that clung to his chest and arms....

Everything around her went soft.

His mouth moved, but she couldn't hear him through the pounding of blood in her ears. Finally, she licked her lips and looked away.

"Hey, are you okay?" He touched her arm, quickly pulling back when she looked at his fingers on her skin. Could he feel that same electric pulse now jump-starting her heart? Did a tingle start in his throat and shoot through his stomach too?

"So my stupid coworkers told my sister that I was bringing my boyfriend to the family anniversary party." She flicked her eyes in his direction again and found him staring at her. "I tried explaining, but my sister, Helene, well." She blew out her breath. "She can be a real piece of work. I could tell her the truth, and she wouldn't believe me at this point."

"I think I can handle it. Believe it or not, I've been someone's boyfriend before."

Cora smiled. "I'm sure you have." She cocked her hip and looked fully at him, struck again by his straight nose and those brilliant white teeth and wow, did he have stars in his eyes?

She cleared her throat, reminding herself that she hadn't gotten up and done fifty pushups for fun. Or to impress Brennan Fuller.

"I'm sure you normally learn things about a woman one at a time," she said.

"Normally, yes."

Core pulled in a deep breath. "Well, this isn't going to be normal, then."

He let his eyes travel from the top of her head to her own booted feet. "I don't think much about you is normal, Cora." His face immediately reddened, and he ducked his head.

Ah, so he'd felt the current between them. Did time seem to swell and stop when he looked at her the way it did for her?

"We'll have to fast-track some things."

He put a ball cap on his head, making his jaw seem slightly squarer than before. "Can you talk and work at the same time?"

"Sure thing."

He nodded toward the parking lot. "I've got loads more bags of bark in my truck. An extra pair of shears. Stuff like that."

She positioned herself at his side, glad when he led her to a normal-sized truck the color of his dark jeans.

He lowered the tailgate and lifted three bags of bark with the words, "You can grab the shears and that bucket."

Cora waited until he'd turned from the truck and then she heaved three bags of bark into her arms too. As she stood a few inches shorter than Brennan, it was quite the stretch to get her arms around the bags, but she hipped them into place and started after him.

When he flung his bags on the ground beside the ones she'd already seen and then turned, his eyes widened. He stumbled forward. "Cora, you're going to hurt yourself."

She let him take a bag of bark, saying, "It's bark. It doesn't weigh that much." Besides she lifted weights every day. The fire equipment the hotshots carried could weigh up to one hundred pounds, and she had to take it with her everywhere.

"How long have you been a firefighter?" he asked, swiping one hand under his hat.

"Nine years." She continued with her story, telling him about her job at Fire House Four in Vernal and her desire to be a hotshot on a national crew.

As she talked, the truck got unloaded, and Brennan finally slipped on a pair of work gloves and clapped his hands.

"So you like fighting fires. Been doing it for a while. You've been here a year, and you want to be a hotshot." He lifted his eyebrows, as if to check to see if he'd gotten it right.

Cora grinned at him, gesturing for him to continue as he handed her a pair of gloves as well.

"Family's in Vernal. Sister named Helene. Her husband is Matt. They have two kids, a boy and a girl. I can't remember their names."

"Doesn't matter," Cora said, impressed he'd remembered as much as he had.

"An older brother named Edgar. He's married to… uh…."

"Dani," Cora supplied.

"Dani, right." He pulled a bucket down to the corner and started pulling microscopic weeds from around the bushes. "They have three kids. All girls."

"Those are the basics, yes." She joined him, starting down about ten feet and intending to work toward him. "So what do I need to know about you? Siblings? Parents still married?"

Brennan sent a booming laugh into the sky, but Cora didn't understand why. She waited for him to quiet, then met his eye with unspoken questions between them.

"You don't know anything about my family." He said it with a sense of awe, his beautiful eyes broadcasting just as much astonishment.

"I know you're a Fuller," she said. "Kent said your family was a founding family of Brush Creek." Which meant he had strong ties here. Strong ties that wouldn't break when she finally got appointed to a hotshot crew.

Doesn't matter, she told herself, plucking another thistle from where it tried to hide right up next to the trunk of the shrub. *This is a temporary arrangement. One week. One party.*

"Right," he said. "Both sets of my grandparents are still alive. I have a great-grandfather still living too. My parents are still married, yes, and I have eight brothers and sisters."

"Eight." Cora coughed, the surprise on her tongue quick and sour. "Wow."

"You don't need to remember all of them," he said. "Two of my older brothers are married, and the sister just younger than me is getting married in a couple of weeks."

"Well, maybe I should know her name," Cora said. "Maybe we'd be friends?" She wasn't sure why she'd phrased it as a question.

"Of all my sisters, Wren is definitely the...." He seemed to fumble for the right word, finally coming up with, "one you'd meet first." He looked away quickly, his attention singular on the weeds now.

"How many brothers?" she asked.

"Three. All older."

"So five sisters."

"All younger."

"Well, that makes it easy, doesn't it?" She threw a beaming smile at him, thrilled when he returned it easily. That conduit between them blinked into existence again, and Cora had the strangest desire to sweep her hand down the side of his face just to feel the strength in his jaw.

Clearing her throat, she dropped her eyes to the

ground. The dirt seemed like a deep, rich chocolate brown, and she sifted it for a moment, trying to get her bearings. She finally got herself back together enough to pull another weed from the ground.

When they met in the flowerbed, they both got up and repositioned themselves to get another section of garden weeded. "So," Cora said, sighing. "Let's do favorites next."

"Favorites?"

"You know, favorite food. Color. What do you like? What do you not like? That kind of thing."

"Don't you think we should work out how we met first?"

"Oh, well, I thought we could just go with the karaoke bar." She met his gaze. "Don't you—I mean—do you—?"

"You think that's romantic enough for your family?" He paused in his work too, his gaze all-assessing and combing her face.

Cora didn't care what her family thought, not about this. "I thought it was pretty romantic," she admitted with the shrug of one shoulder. "I mean, you went and talked to my friends while I was singing." She ducked her head, wishing she'd brought a hat she could hide behind.

"You have a beautiful voice," he said, drawing her attention back to him. "Like an angel."

Cora had never been called an angel before, and she rather liked the way he looked at her with that adorable glint in his eye. She also had no idea what to do with these soft feelings inside her or why she had the urge to know everything about Brennan—not just what she needed to get through the party. But everything about him, so she could decide if their lives could intertwine and become one.

Startled by the treacherous path her thoughts had taken, she shook her head and got back to work. She needed Brennan for the next week, that was all.

She certainly didn't need him to worm his way into the soft parts of her heart. She didn't even have soft parts of her heart, and it would be better for both of them if they focused on putting on a good performance for the party and then getting back to their real lives.

Chapter 4

Brennan spent church obsessing over the exotic brunette who had talked his ear off the day before. He had the fruity smell of her perfume memorized, along with an insane amount of information that seemed to slip through his mind like water through a sieve.

On Saturday morning, he enjoyed the rare luxury of sleeping in, only to awaken with a start. He scrambled for his phone to make sure he hadn't missed his alarm. He sagged back against his pillow when he realized he hadn't. Not even close.

So maybe his dreams had been filled with the warmth of Cora's hand in his, her hair brushing his forearm as she tipped her head back and laughed.

"Don't be stupid," he told himself as he stepped into the shower. "Today will be the last day you see her." After all, the party was today, and then that was that.

Cora had made it very clear over the past week that their relationship ended when the party did.

Brennan must've been imagining the fireworks between them whenever their eyes met. He hadn't imagined the way his mouth turned dry and his pulse pounded. But his symptoms were obviously his alone, though she laughed at his jokes, gushed over the chicken parmesan he'd made from scratch, and taken to Sybil like they were bosom buddies.

He knew that she liked thrills, from riding a motorcycle to rock climbing to fighting fires. He knew she had strength in her lithe body and wasn't afraid to show him she could do as much as he could.

She'd skipped college and had several boyfriends over the years. She hadn't been super forthcoming about her past relationships, but Brennan supposed it wasn't any of his business. They weren't really dating, after all. That had been made clear too.

And yet, somehow, Brennan had allowed himself to think they could. At some point. Maybe after the party, he could text her and ask her out to a real dinner. Maybe she'd say yes.

Brennan dressed with care, wearing a pair of gray golf shorts and a navy, white, and black striped polo. He brushed his teeth twice and tried to feed Sybil three times.

When Cora's bike rumbled into his driveway, he grabbed his wallet and keys and headed out the front door. The sight of the leggy brunette climbing off the motorcycle pressed his pulse into a frenzy, and he was struck dumb as he stared.

She took off her helmet and shook out her hair. It tumbled over her shoulders in brilliant waves, and she rested the helmet against her hip and grinned at him.

His ridiculous lips smiled back. Thankfully, his legs remembered it was time to go and he met her at the passenger door to the truck. "You bringing the helmet?"

She tossed the helmet onto the bench seat after he opened the door. "Sure, why not?"

Brennan liked this fun, flirty side of her. He'd seen a more withdrawn Cora as well, and a serious, driven version as well.

She chattered as they drove down Main Street, bypassing all the old brick buildings that lent Brush Creek so much of its charm. Vernal was the same way, with historical markers seemingly on every corner. Though not old by the world's standards by any means, the cities and towns here in eastern Utah reminded Brennan that life didn't have to be made of steel and glass to be wonderful.

The helmet rode on the seat between them, and Brennan didn't like that. Cora quieted as they approached Vernal, and that set his nerves on high alert too. She directed him left and right until they pulled into a driveway that already held two minivans.

"Great," she muttered. "Everyone's here already."

"We're not late, are we?" He cut a quick glance at his watch.

"No." She sighed. "I guess I didn't tell you about my family's insane time thing." She turned her beautiful eyes on him, and Brennan's breath hitched in his chest. "If they say eleven o'clock, you're late if you show up at ten-thirty." She shook her head, a half-smile dancing across her mouth.

Brennan chuckled, the sound easy and easing some of the tension between them. But his palms felt slick and his anxiety quivered near the surface. He wasn't a great conversationalist, and he felt certain he was about to forget some very important detail that would ruin everything with Cora.

He unbuckled and got out of the truck, meeting Cora at the corner on her side. The curtain in the huge front window fluttered, which meant someone was already watching. He wasn't sure if Cora had seen it or not. Easily, simply, like he'd done it a thousand times before, he slipped his hand into hers.

As a charge as powerful as lightning bolted up his arm, he tilted his head and brushed his lips against her temple. "You ready for this?" He actually smiled as he said it, as if they were sharing a truly intimate moment before facing six adults and five children, all of whom surely had perfectly good eyes and would be able to see this scam for what it was.

Cora looked up at him, and Brennan may have been imagining a lot of things. But there was no mistaking the edge of heat in her eyes right now. Automatically, his fingers squeezed hers. She gripped his hand too and nodded.

Buoyed up by the prospect of extending their relationship past this party, Brennan faced the house again. "All right, then." He took the first step, gently towing her with him. "Helene and Matt. Edgar and Dani. Chris and Laura." He'd at least get the names right.

The front door opened, and her mother emerged wearing a black cocktail dress that certainly didn't fit at a Saturday afternoon backyard barbeque—what Cora had prepped him for.

She wore a sundress, sure. But the blue, yellow, and white dress was a far cry from the evening wear her mother had on.

"Cora," she said, smiling though it felt a touch on the predatory side to Brennan. "Come in, come in." She went first and Brennan waited for Cora to follow her. They embraced, and no matter what Cora said about her family, Brennan could see the affection her mother had for her.

When they parted, Cora smoothed her hands over her thighs to right her dress and looked at Brennan. "Mom, this is my boyfriend, Brennan. Brennan, my mother, Laura."

Her physical assessment of him happened in the blink of an eye, but Brennan still felt underdressed and way out of his league. "Ma'am." He nodded at her, wishing he had a hat he could tip.

"I've heard so little about you," she said, tossing a disdainful glance toward Cora.

"Mom," she warned, rolling her eyes as if to say *See? This is what I have to put up with.*

"Well, I've heard a lot about you," Brennan said, the words flowing easily out of his mouth. "Cora tells me the trees along the west side of the house were planted when you moved in. And then one for each child as they were born."

Surprise crossed Laura's face. While technically what he'd said wasn't about her mother at all, he could tell it meant something to her.

"I'd like to see them," he said. "See, I'm a landscaper."

"A landscaper?" her mother repeated.

"He owns his own business," Cora jumped in, almost wedging herself between Brennan and her mom. "They're really successful. They have contracts with the city and the school district, as well as do residential stuff."

Brennan put on a smile that was actually genuine. Listening to Cora talk about him like she knew him was satisfying. He reminded himself that she knew some things *about* him, but that she didn't actually know him. "So I'd love to see the trees."

"Right this way." Laura pointed through a doorway. "Everyone's in the backyard already. Did you bring the buns, Cora?"

Her shoulders stiffened, and Brennan's heart skipped over a beat. He hadn't seen any food. Hadn't even known they'd been assigned to bring something.

"I forgot," Cora said with a groan.

Her mom paused and turned back before entering a mudroom. "Well, how can we have burgers and pulled pork without buns?"

"I'll go grab some," Brennan said. He'd been to Vernal plenty of times; he could find a grocery store.

"Nonsense." Laura's hand curled around his forearm, drawing him into the mudroom with her. "Cora was supposed to bring the buns. She can go get them." She arched one brow in Cora's direction that spoke volumes.

Helpless and not sure what to say, Brennan fished in his pocket for the keys to his truck. "I can go with her."

"Oh, we've all been *dying* to meet you," Laura said. "She'll be gone for twenty minutes. She'll be fine. Right, Cora?"

Cora looked like she could burn this place to the ground with a well-placed look. "Right, Mother." She fisted the keys in a way that looked painful and spun on her heel, marching toward the front door without a glance in Brennan's direction.

He watched her go, that light dress complementing her tanned skin and dark hair. For a fleeting moment, he actually wondered if she'd come back. Then Laura opened the back door, and Brennan had no choice but to follow her to meet the rest of Cora's family—alone.

Helene was a younger version of her mother, with the same brown hair and round face. Same chocolately brown eyes that saw far more than just what was on the surface. No wonder Cora had given him so many details about her life.

Her father turned from the grill, and Brennan instantly saw where Cora's darker hair and skin came from. Chris smiled with those same gold-infused eyes, and out of everyone Brennan met in the next few minutes, he liked her father the best.

Cora's nieces and nephew played in the secluded yard, and Brennan really did enjoy the huge trees on the west side of the house. They created a natural fence line, provided privacy from the neighbor's nearby, and drenched the backyard in shade.

With the small deck and paved patio, the yard was an inviting place to be, and Brennan relaxed a little bit. At least until Helene said, "So how did you two meet?"

"Oh, uh." Brennan picked up a plastic water bottle and twisted the lid before launching into the karaoke story.

"Cora sang?" Laura perched on the edge of the bench, her dress bunched tightly around her knees. "That doesn't sound like her."

"Her buddies had to practically drag her up the steps," he said, remembering her struggle with Kent and Charlie—at least until she'd seen him. Then she'd sort of gone limp, and they'd gotten her on the stage fairly easily after that.

He remembered the way she sang right to him, her voice an intoxicating drug to his whole system. "It was just sort of like...magic." He sighed, only realizing how soft and wistful it made him sound after he'd done it.

Both Helene and Laura stared at him like he'd grown four heads in a matter of seconds. He cleared his throat. "Anyway—"

"When did this happen?" Helene asked. "Seems like Cora would've mentioned...magically meeting a handsome man."

"Oh, I don't know," he said, realizing he and Cora hadn't exactly worked out the details of their relationship. Or had they? The sun shone so hotly overhead, and Brennan wiped his brow. "I think it was near the end of March. I don't get out to the karaoke bar much, but my brothers wanted to go."

"Cora goes all the time," Laura said, a definite note of disdain in her voice.

"Yeah, she likes it." Brennan wasn't actually sure if that was true, or she'd been dragged there by her firemen buddies. They hadn't discussed her karaoke habits that much. Or at all.

"There's so much about her I don't understand." Laura frowned, the lines deep between her eyes. "Like the firefighting. What woman does that?" She looked at him as if Brennan would confirm that it was a ridiculous career for a woman.

"I think it's sexy," he blurted, unsure of where the words had come from. All he knew was that a burning desire to defend her burned through him like a wildfire ravaging a forest. "She's good at it too. She's only been in

Brush Creek for a year, and she's the captain of her unit."

"There's only one unit in Brush Creek, isn't there?" Edgar spoke in a low, deep voice, smooth and without emotion, but it still felt like he was undermining his sister.

"Right. One unit. It's a small department. I think there's eight of them. Cora and seven men. And the Fire Chief." He took a long drink of his water, wondering how long it had been since Cora had left. His stomach grumbled for lunch, but they couldn't eat without the buns. "She seems to really enjoy it, and becoming Captain of seven men isn't easy."

"Hmm." Edgar looked over Brennan's shoulder to the yard.

"What do you do?" he asked her brother, a note of accusation in his voice. He tamped it down, reminding himself this was just a show. Cora planned to text her sister in a couple of weeks and tell her things with Brennan just weren't working out.

Before her holier-than-thou brother could answer, Helene said, "She did tell you she wants to be a hotshot, right?"

Brennan nodded. "She mentioned it, yes."

"You know that means she's out in the wilderness for weeks on end," Laura added, not bothering to phrase her words as a question.

"I'm not really familiar with what they do, no." Brennan couldn't help looking at his phone. Cora had been gone for seven minutes, and he was drowning without her. "But I'm sure we'll cross that bridge when we come to it."

"She's doing all the physical tests in September." Helene lifted her chin as if she and Cora had personally planned her training schedule and when she'd apply for the hotshots crew.

Laura shook her head. "You didn't see her, but she looks so...manly. Too buff."

Brennan almost choked. Cora was anything but manly or masculine. She had female curves he may have stared at a little too long more than once as they'd gotten together this week. With high cheekbones and a slender neck, Cora had rendered him breathless every time he'd seen her.

"See? He agrees."

"No," he said quickly, his face heating. "No, I don't agree. She's beautiful."

"She's too thin and her muscles bulge." Laura glared at him, daring him to contradict her again. "You'll see," she said to Helene and Edgar, who both watched him with laser-sharp gazes.

"She likes to run," Brennan said. "But she's not too thin. She can lift three bags of bark. Five cubic feet bags of bark. She hauled tree limbs like they were sticks." Working with her on her off-days this past week had been the most exhilarating time of Brennan's life. "She's a hard worker." He shook his head, not quite believing how critical her mother was being of her, especially when Cora wasn't here to defend herself. "She's not too thin, and her muscles don't bulge."

He looked away from her family to watch the children, but he still caught the elbow Helene threw into Edgar's side. They both looked dubious, and Brennan couldn't sit there for another second.

"Excuse me." He made a hasty escape inside the house, his heart pounding and his brain buzzing with anger. It was hard to think, but he made it into the bathroom and pulled out his phone.

Text me when you get back, he typed out to Cora. *I'll come meet you in the driveway.*

Ugh, she texted back immediately. *Is everything okay?*

He looked at himself in the mirror and found himself red-faced and upset. *Sort of.*

Sort of?

How much longer will you be?

Waiting to check out now.

Brennan waited a few more seconds and then flushed the toilet, just in case someone had followed him inside. He wouldn't put it past Laura—or Helene, for that matter. Instead of returning to the backyard, he went out the front door and planted himself on the steps. How he was going to make it through another five hours of this, he didn't know.

His truck ambled toward the house, and Cora pulled into the driveway, her eyes singular on his. He stood, his heart racing as he felt the weight of her family's eyes on him. He wasn't sure if they were watching or not, and he didn't check behind him to see.

He just marched toward Cora, who got out of the truck to meet him. "What happened?"

"Nothing." Feeling bold and powerful and completely out of control, Brennan swept his arms around her, dipped his head, and kissed her like he'd never kissed a woman before.

Her surprise came through in the unyielding nature of her mouth. Then, as if by that same magic he'd described earlier, her hands drifted up his arms and across his shoulders, setting fire to his skin beneath his shirt. Her nails gently scratched as she moved her fingers into his hair, and Brennan couldn't control the shiver of desire and delight that tripped through all his bones.

Her mouth softened and welcomed his, and Brennan prolonged the kiss as his anger and anxiety seeped away.

CHAPTER 5

ora had been gone for seventeen minutes. She wasn't even sure what kind of buns she'd bought. She'd grabbed the first four bags she'd seen and raced toward the checkout.

Something must've happened in those seventeen minutes, because she'd found Brennan sitting on the front steps, alone.

And now she was kissing him. Admittedly, she hadn't kissed a man in years, but wow. This was by far the most sensual and passionate kiss she'd had since the first couple of months of her marriage—which she still hadn't told Brennan about.

His hands burned through the fabric of her dress, and everything in her screamed at her to pull away and end this show. But she couldn't, and she kept kissing him —at least until her mother cleared her throat.

Cora pulled back then, and Brennan turned to reveal

her mom and Helene, both of them standing there watching. Cora tucked herself into his chest, her thundering heart matching the cadence of his.

"Did you get the buns?" her mom asked in a voice made of acid. "We're waiting on you."

Cora wanted to toss the bags of bread at her mother and get out of town. She wasn't sure what she'd done that had sparked so much ire in her mom and sister.

Yes, you do, she thought. And it wasn't something she'd done, but rather something she hadn't. She hadn't included them in her life since the divorce. They'd all loved Brandt so much, and none of them understood why he'd left.

Cora didn't quite understand that either, only that she wasn't enough for him and the result was him filing for divorce and leaving town, all in the same day. Her mom and sister had come to the same conclusion—Cora was flawed and had driven Brandt away.

Since then, she'd felt like a stranger in her own family. It was easier to avoid family functions like this one, and Brush Creek sat far enough from Vernal that she couldn't just pop down to see them on a Sunday afternoon after church.

You know, if Cora went to church. Which, most of the time, she didn't. Another disappointment for her mother to dwell on.

Brennan stepped away from her to retrieve the buns. He handed them to Helene and her mom, and they left.

"What in the world?" she hissed as they went

through the garage to get to the backyard. She searched his face, but he kept his eyes glued toward her family's retreating forms.

"Brennan," she said, finally drawing his attention to her. His glorious eyes devoured her, and she liked it. She'd had men look at her like this before, and she'd never liked it.

"Sorry," he said.

"You *kissed* me."

"As if I didn't know." He touched his lips as if reliving the experience.

"What happened?" she asked again.

"They were talking about you, and I just...I just got stressed."

Cora sighed, wishing she had pockets to stuff her hands into. She hated this dress. All dresses, as a general rule. To see her mom strutting around in one like she was attending the Oscars made Cora's head pound in a way that no painkillers could ever touch.

"Well, that's going to make things more difficult."

"What is? Me kissing you? Which, by the way, not sure if you noticed, but you kissed me back."

And she'd liked that too. Wanted to do it again, in fact. Shoving the thought from her mind with all of her willpower, she turned to face the house. "I guess I didn't tell you that I'm a complete disappointment to my mother."

"You failed to mention that, yes."

"And Helene goes along with it, because it makes her feel better about her own, unfulfilled life."

"Her husband isn't even here," Brennan noted. "Edgar's wife is here, and all the kids. But Matt didn't come."

"Really?" Cora's eyebrows went up. "I wonder why." She put her hand in Brennan's again, liking how it fit there, like his hand was just one size bigger than hers and had been made to protect her. "Probably another reason why she's so vitriolic toward you. You're a reminder of what she doesn't have here."

"Vitriolic. Wow, big word." He chuckled, nudging her into a walk with his shoulder. "She said you were too skinny and too masculine. I disagreed."

Cora paused at the mouth of the garage. "You disagreed, huh?"

He gazed down on her, a definite edge in his eyes that hinted at more than a charade. "I think you're gorgeous. Beautiful. Strong. Powerful." He brought her closer, and she inhaled the stringent, manly scent of his cologne. "I think watching you carry three bags of bark is sexy, and that's a word I never use."

A ruddy blush crept into his face, but he didn't duck his head or look away from her. "So maybe I wanted to kiss you to show them how feminine I found you. Or maybe I just wanted to kiss you."

Her head swam with the heat of his body, the near-ness of him, and everything he was saying. She had no response, because she hadn't expected this to be the problem she'd find when she returned.

True, her family could be cruel. But she'd been dealing with that for four years. She had defenses against it.

But she had no defense against Brennan and the wonderful things he'd said. Nothing to ward off a kiss that emotional and powerful.

"Maybe you'd sit by me at church tomorrow?" He touched his lips to her forehead and dragged his nose along the side of her face. Her eyes closed as she stilled, tensed, waited for his mouth to claim hers again.

"I don't go to church," she whispered.

"Ever?" His breath mingled with hers, dangerously close and terribly far away at the same time.

"I mean, I guess I go sometimes."

"How about tomorrow, then?"

She gave one nod of her head without thinking. All she knew was she felt something for Brennan she hadn't felt in a long, long time, and she liked it. Liked the vibrant, alive feeling it gave her, the same way racing through the night on her motorcycle did.

With her eyes still closed, she tilted her head, her mouth catching the edge of his. Aligning quickly, easily, she initiated a much slower, softer kiss this second time around. It was just as wonderful and just as life-changing as the first time.

———

APPARENTLY HER MOTHER and sister had gotten their nastiness out while she was gone, because the rest of the party went just fine. She wanted to ask Helene why Matt hadn't come, but in the end, she didn't want to cause any ripples.

So she kept her head down, spoke when spoken to, and tried to keep her father involved in the conversations. Her mom always acted better with her dad around, and when he got up to clean the grill, Cora said, "Well, we need to get back to Brush Creek."

She stood, her hand still in Brennan's. He'd stayed right at her side, and he was a great conversationalist, good at asking questions that required long answers, and good at offering help when cleaning up.

"So soon?" her mom asked.

They'd been there for three hours. "It's a long drive."

"It's an hour."

Cora started to sit, trying to get back under that radar. But Brennan said, "Well, I have an appointment this evening, so we really do need to go a bit early." He flashed a look at Cora, who straightened again.

Cora hugged her family while Brennan waited by the back door. He shook hands with her father, and they made their escape. She finally took her first full breath in hours once she was seated in Brennan's truck.

"I'm so sorry," she said, turning toward him and taking her motorcycle helmet onto her lap. The shiny red surface showed her face back to her, and she recognized her anxiety and annoyance.

"It's fine." He drove with one hand draped over the steering wheel. "I liked your dad."

Cora nodded, still studying herself in the helmet. "I like my dad too. He didn't blame me after—" She cut herself off, shocked she was about to utter her ex-husband's name.

"How often do you visit them?" he asked.

"Three or four times a year."

"Mm hm." He glanced at her and she looked up from her reflection. "My family is intense too," he said. "There are a lot of us, so just getting everyone together causes a fair bit of stress."

Cora leaned her head back and closed her eyes. "I'm sure it is. I'm still sorry. That was way more than I should've asked you to do."

He said something, but she couldn't catch what as he'd spoken too softly. She let her mind drift and the next thing she knew, Brennan had said her name and touched her arm.

"We're home," he said. The golden sun shone behind him, haloing him in beautiful light. Her lips lifted into a smile, and in her sleepy state, she thought he was the most handsome man she'd ever met.

"Hey, you."

He smiled at her too, and that magical conduit that had first bound them together formed again. Brennan cleared his throat, further waking Cora from her cat nap. She straightened and bent for her motorcycle helmet, which had fallen to the floor at some point during the drive.

"So," he said. "I was still wondering about church tomorrow. You never said if you'd come or not."

Cora's pulse skipped a beat and then another one. "I haven't been in a while."

"That's okay," he said. "I go to the red brick building right on Main Street. It's an hour—tops—in the summer, and I'll even cook you lunch after." His eyes shone with an inner light that intrigued her.

So she said, "Sure, church. What time is that?"

"Ten-thirty. Do you have to work tomorrow?"

"I'm on the dinner shift," she said. "So I have to go into the station about three and make dinner for every-one. I'll sleep there tomorrow night too."

"What do you make for dinner?"

She chuckled at the thought of cooking for a dozen men. "I order pizza when it's my turn," she said. "I'm not much of a cook."

"I'm not bad," he said. "What do you like?"

"Whatever you make, I'll eat," she said, giving him what she hoped was a flirty smile. It worked, because he ducked his head, that sexy blush coloring his face again. She'd had plenty of practice with her flirting. That wasn't the problem. It was everything that came after the first flirtatious date.

Her lungs seized. Was this party a date? Would sitting by him at church be considered a date? And so what if they were? She liked Brennan. Liked holding his hand. Really liked kissing him.

With the memory of his lips on hers, she unbuckled and slipped from his truck. He followed her to her motorcycle, where she paused to pull her hair into a ponytail. "Thanks for coming with me," she said.

"Once you got back from the store, I thought it went fine." He slid his fingers up her arm, curling them behind her neck. His touch sent shattering sparks through her, but when he tipped her head back and dipped his head toward hers, she froze.

He did too. Their eyes met, and though Cora wanted to kiss him again, she wasn't sure what that made her.

"You don't have to."

"Have to?" He straightened.

"We're not at the party." She giggled with a nervous undertone and backed up. "There's no one to convince."

Brennan frowned and fell back a step too. "So... where does that leave us?"

Cora hadn't really been thinking in terms of us—at least not until he'd kissed her in front of her mom and sister.

"I like you," he blurted.

"Maybe...I mean, maybe we could just...go out a little. You know, for real."

"Right." He nodded and rubbed his palm along the back of his head. "Get to really know each other, not just know *about* each other."

"Exactly." She put her helmet on her head and

fastened the chin strap. "Thank you for going with me today."

He nodded and stepped back as she swung herself onto her bike, fired it up, and left him standing in his driveway.

"It's for the best," she muttered to herself as she faced her bike into the sunset. Though she wanted to kiss him again, Cora was also less than sure about truly starting a relationship with him. With anyone, for that matter. But especially Brennan Fuller, as he indeed lit something in her that had been burnt out since her marriage had ended, years ago.

And if she allowed that fire to spark and flame, then what?

"Then the whole world will be blazing before you know it," she told herself, turning south again and heading down the same road she'd just come back to town on. And Cora, as a firefighter, did her darndest to keep the world from burning down.

So if she set Brennan on a shelf until she could figure out what to do with him, her world could go on as normal.

As she pulled into Beaverton and stopped at the best taco joint within fifty miles, she knew her version of normal had changed the moment Brennan had molded his lips to hers.

CHAPTER 6

Brennan stood on the sidewalk outside the red brick church, baking in his collared shirt and bright blue tie. At ten-twenty-nine, he heard the rumble of Cora's motorcycle, beyond glad when she turned into the lot and pulled right up to the sidewalk where he stood. She moved with the grace of a cat as she dismounted and removed her helmet. She did that head toss to let her hair down, and the motion rendered him dry-mouthed just as it had last time.

"Morning." She flashed him a smile, but didn't step into his personal space to take his hand.

"Morning." He turned and opened the door so she could enter.

"Where do you usually sit?" She stepped with all the confidence of someone who'd been attending church for their entire life, but Brennan suspected it was a front.

Sure enough, she paused at the doors to the chapel, her head swiveling from one side to the other.

She fiddled with the hem of her shirt, a bright orange blouse that made her hair seem like the color of midnight.

He pointed to the right. "Back row," he whispered.

Cora moved in that direction, and Brennan sat on the end of the row next to her just as the pastor got up and started speaking. Brennan couldn't concentrate, nothing new for church. He attended every week, because his mother expected it. He wished he could be as brave as his sister Dawn, who hadn't darkened the door of a church in at least three years.

But Brennan knew of his mother's disappointment, and besides, he felt more peace and hope in his life when he attended church. Even when he simply sat in the pews and absorbed the energy in the building.

That was all he was able to do today, as distracted with Cora's fruity perfume as he was. He also spent a bit of time obsessing over the beef bolognese he'd spent most of the morning putting together. It should be boiling away in a low oven, getting nice and browned and deep in flavor. He'd perfected his bolognese over the years, and if it didn't impress Cora, he didn't know what would.

He wanted to hold her hand, but after yesterday's blunder in his driveway, he wanted her to make the first move more. So he kept his hands to himself and pretended to listen to Pastor Peters until the choir stood to sing the last song. Then he nudged her and nodded toward the exit.

She reached for her purse and followed him out, looping the strap over her shoulder and neck. "So I'll meet you at your place."

"Sure." He actually followed her, as he'd actually had to park in the lot while she'd sidled up to the sidewalk.

Once inside, his small house felt even cozier with Cora there with him. She'd been here before, but somehow this was different. The awkwardness between them had fully bloomed, and Brennan wondered why their relationship had shifted from the easiness of last week.

He pulled the cast iron pot out of the oven and stirred the bolognese while Cora drew in a deep breath. "Smells amazing."

"I hope it is." He slid it back into the oven and filled a pot with water. "So, I'm prepared to tell you a couple of things about me," he said. "How do you feel about doing the same?"

He caught the way she swallowed, saw the sliver of fear in her eyes before she blinked and erased it. Still, she nodded, and he switched the pot from the sink to the stove and put the flame underneath it.

"Great." He leaned against the counter and faced her. "I don't really like working for my family's business."

Her eyebrows lifted. "No?"

"No."

"Why do you do it then?"

He inhaled deliberately and exhaled. "Duty? Obligation? Because I don't want to rock the boat?"

"And all your siblings work for A Jack of All Trades, right?"

"Yes, all of them."

"So if you didn't, if you broke the mold...." She lifted one shoulder. "You'd be left out."

"I'm already overlooked as it is," he admitted. Once he said it, something broke free in his soul. He'd never told anyone that he was the forgotten one in the Fuller family. It felt nice to share his emotions with someone, even if Cora couldn't quite understand.

"I believe it. With that many brothers and sisters." She leaned her elbows on the counter, her eyes never leaving his. "So what would you do if you could do anything you wanted?"

"I don't know."

"Sure you do."

"I really don't."

"You haven't thought about it?"

Brennan added a healthy dose of salt to the water. "I mean, I guess I have."

"So? What would you do?"

"Landscaping is what I grew up doing. Painting. Fixing household appliances. That kind of thing."

"It's probably a good job," she said.

"I get by."

"From what I can tell, you do more than get by." She glanced around his house as if he had precious stones on display. "Granite countertops. Cherry cabinets. Stainless steel appliances. It's nice."

Brennan looked around his house, surprised by her assessment. "We know a lot of people," he said. "We usually get everything at a reduced price."

"That must be nice," she said.

Brennan didn't like this line of conversation, so he said, "I think I'd like to be an architect."

"You like to design things?"

"Yes."

Cora tilted her head and studied him with a bright sparkle in her eye. He chuckled and asked, "What?"

"Have you heard of a landscape architect?"

"No."

"They work with city planners. Universities. Big businesses who are concerned about the environment and making their campuses green in all senses of the word. That kind of stuff."

"How do you know?"

"I took several environmental classes in the year I went to college. I was interested in being an environmentalist. Then I joined the fire academy and took a different path."

"You went to college?"

She smiled and tossed her ponytail over her shoulder. "Does that count as one of my things to tell you today?"

"Sure." He wasn't sure why he was surprised to hear Cora had attended a university. Only that a strange sensation had pulled through him, and it felt a lot like... jealousy.

"I've always wanted to go to college," he said quietly. He'd never told anyone that little tidbit either. His oldest brother had gone to college in Salt Lake City, earning a bachelor's degree in business. Wren had also gone and earned a degree in business management. She managed the business, so it made sense. And Milton was the first in line to take over the whole company when their father retired, so his degree was warranted too.

But Brennan's need to go to college was nil. It had never even been discussed. The men in his family took care of handyman jobs, landscaping, and construction. The women did all the cleaning.

"You should go then," Cora said.

"It's not that easy." The lid on the pasta pot clanked, and he ripped open the package of linguine and dropped it into the boiling water. He stirred it, his thoughts rotating just as violently.

"Why not?"

"Because," he said like that answered everything.

"You can afford it, can't you?"

"Monetarily, yes."

"What? You can't get time off work?"

He faced her again, a vein of electricity coursing through him. It felt a lot like...possibility. "No," he said. "I can't get time off work. I manage all the landscaping for the city and the school district. Just me. If I go off to college—" Just the thought had him shaking his head. It was impossible.

"If I go off to college, who will do that?"

"You have three other brothers."

"Who are already busy enough as it is." He dismissed what she was about to say with a wave of his hand. "It's fine. I'm happy enough."

Cora's mouth snapped shut, clearly flummoxed that *happy enough* was good enough for him. Brennan frowned too. When had that happened? When had he accepted *happy enough* as his norm?

"Your turn," he practically barked. "Tell me something I don't know about you."

Her face blanked, and the timer on the linguine went off, saving her from having to say anything. He busied himself with putting together the bolognese with the noodles, and he served the two of them at the bar.

She graced him with a soft smile and twirled a heaping forkful of noodles into her mouth. A moan came from her throat as her eyes rolled back in her head.

"This is the best thing I've ever put in my mouth." She took another bite, and satisfaction soared through Brennan. If he couldn't impress her with his life choices, at least he had bolognese.

They ate with small talk in the background, and the fun, easy way of being together returned.

He hadn't realized how unhappy he was with his life until the moment he'd spoken the words "happy enough," but he wasn't sure what he was supposed to do about it now. He finished eating and started packing up a big container of food for Gramps and Grams.

"So I usually go visit my grandparents on Sunday," he said. "You up for that?"

She put her plate—scraped clean—in the sink. "You met my overbearing siblings and mother. I think I can handle a set of grandparents."

Sybil waddled into the kitchen from where she'd been sleeping in his bedroom. She seemed to understand the word "visit," and she always wanted to go play with Pops.

He picked up the linguine bolognese and pointed to the back door. "All right, Syb. Let's go." He told Cora about his grandparents and their dog on the way over, ending with, "Just yell what you want them to really hear. They're sort of deaf."

She laughed, but kept her legs crossed and herself clear at the other end of the bench seat in his truck. He'd seen plenty of girlfriends ride right next to their boyfriends in a pickup truck, but Cora didn't really seem like that kind of woman. After all, he didn't know any woman who drove a motorcycle and not a sensible sedan. Had never met a female firefighter before either. She wasn't typical, and Brennan wondered if he'd been looking in all the wrong places all these years.

Obviously, he told himself as he pulled up to Gramps's house. Cora climbed out and waited for Sybil to follow her. The basset hound had completely betrayed him, falling in love with Cora seemingly as fast as Brennan had.

You're not in love with her, he chastised himself as he led her up the front walk. "Gramps," he called as he opened the door. "I brought you something to eat." He glanced over his shoulder at Cora, who stepped into the house and gazed around at the old wallpaper, the nearly shag carpet in the formal living room.

"Grams?" Brennan walked past the dining room on his right and the hallway on his left, which led to a few bedrooms, and into the kitchen. "Pops?"

He pushed into the garage. "Huh. Their car is here."

"They're out back." Cora pointed through the sliding glass door behind the round table in the kitchen where his grandparents normally ate.

He stepped to her side and peered out the glass to find Gramps and Grams working in the yard.

"They're so cute," Cora said, affection obvious in her voice.

Brennan slid open the door and let Sybil teeter through first. Pops barked for all he was worth and made a beeline for the other dog. Gramps turned, his face lighting up when he saw Brennan.

"I brought bolognese," he said, lifting the container.

Grams pulled off one of her leather gloves as she shuffled toward him. "Bolognese. My favorite."

Brennan bent down and gave her a hug, taking the bush shears from her when she handed them to him. "Have you guys had lunch?"

"Just grilled cheese sandwiches," she said.

"They were burnt," Gramps practically yelled.

"That's because someone turned the burner to a nine when I said six," Grams yelled back at him. "Come in, come in," she said. She'd taken two steps toward the back door when she spotted Cora. "Oh."

That about summed it up. Brennan hadn't told Cora all about his empty dating past, but he'd said he hadn't been out with anyone significant recently. She didn't need to know that "recently" meant "the last five years."

She probably needed to know now.

"Hey, yeah," Brennan said. "So this is Cora Wesley. She's...." He had no idea how to classify her. And why should he have to? "We're working together."

Not entirely true, but not entirely false either. He watched her for her reaction, and a slight flutter stole across her eyebrows. She wiped it away quickly and extended her hand for Grams to shake.

"This the woman you ditched me for last weekend?" Gramps asked, his voice so loud it made Brennan cringe.

Cora's attention shot to them, and Brennan chuckled and shrugged. "I guess so, Gramps." He indicated his grandparents. "Cora, this is Gramps and Grams, Daryl and Ebony Fuller. My father's parents."

"Nice to meet you both. Did you know Brennan is an excellent cook?"

"Yes," Gramps said, pushing past her. "We did."

Brennan rolled his eyes. "Don't mind him. He likes to put on a grumpy act when he meets new people." He gestured for her to go first, and she turned. Grams fell in step with her, and he noticed Cora slow hers to match the older woman's. Brennan's heart softened at Cora's kindness, and he paused to watch them go inside together, already chatting like old friends.

Grams had that affect on people, which was exactly why Brennan had brought Cora to meet his grandparents. Then he'd be able to get their opinion on her and ask advice for what to do.

So he was woefully out of practice when it came to women. He should've known that when he kissed her right in front of her family, without warning, without asking, and without really knowing much about her.

A bead of sweat formed on his forehead, and he headed for the air conditioned house, marveling at how much he had to think about after only a couple of hours with Cora. A real relationship with her—could he have one?

A new job, doing something that actually interested him—could that become a reality?

He honestly had no idea about either one, but he really, really wanted to find out.

Chapter 7

Cora showed up at Station Two carrying six pizza boxes. "Sorry I'm late," she called up the stairs before taking them as quickly as she could and maintain her grip on the Philly cheesesteak, all-meat, and Alfredo Hawaiian concoctions she'd spent good money on.

Charlie met her at the top of the steps. "There you are. Haven't seen you all weekend." He took the boxes, and Cora turned around to get the rest of the food out of the back of Brennan's truck.

"Been busy. Family party, remember?" She ducked back outside and accepted the bag with 2-liter soda bottles and the big salad she'd ordered. She always got that for herself, hoping one of the men would eat it too. Usually one or two took pity on her and scooped a few leaves of lettuce onto their plates before drowning the salad in ranch dressing.

"Come on up," she said, her heartbeat quivering as it tried to pump blood through her body.

"I'm coming up?" Brennan stared at her, expecting something serious from her. He'd asked her to share something important from her life, but it had never come up. They'd talked about his career and she hated hearing the sad tone he'd used when he talked about his job and his unrealized dreams of going to college.

But he'd perked up at his grandparent's house, and Cora had admired that strong relationship. Gramps made her laugh, and Grams gave her the unconditional love Cora craved from her own mother. Cora had felt more at home in their home in a matter of minutes than she'd felt in her childhood home in half a decade.

"I kinda like you." Cora grinned at him, glad when his feet shifted and he flushed. "Everyone will grill me mercilessly about you anyway. Might as well give them something to talk about, right?" She bumped him with her hip and added, "So grab the rest of those pizzas, and let's go."

Her pulse accelerated as she climbed the steps for the second time, and she told herself it was simply because of the steepness of the stairs. She entered the common room, where someone had set up the tables for the pizza. Charlie had just slapped a stack of paper plates on the table and swung his attention toward her.

"Salad," she announced. "Soda." She scanned the room to the chorus of Brennan's footsteps, noticing that all the men were there, waiting to be fed. Of course they were. It was Sunday afternoon—*boring*—and they knew she'd bring pizza.

Brennan reached the top of the steps and Cora pulled the plastic bowl of salad from the bag with trembling fingers. Kent took the pizzas from Brennan with a hearty, "Hey, man," and put them on the table.

Cora basked in the silence that never seemed to descend on Station Two. "So this is Brennan Fuller," she said. "I think most of you know him." She suddenly understood how hard it was to introduce him, as they hadn't defined their relationship. Cora despised labels anyway, preferring to have some wiggle room when it came to who she was to someone else.

And maybe she simply wasn't ready to admit she was in a real relationship with a man. She'd spent so long denying herself such pleasures, dedicating herself to a different path than where she'd been before.

Brennan grinned at her, a knowing glint in his eye. He waved to the group of men advancing slowly toward the table. They wouldn't attack the food until Cora gave the go-ahead, and not only because she was their Captain. But because their curiosity sometimes overwhelmed their never-ending need to eat.

"So I'll call you later," he said, stepping over to her. He spoke loud enough to be heard by everyone but not so loud it was obvious he was trying to be heard. He swept his lips along her cheek, moved back, and waved to the men again before disappearing down the steps.

Cora absently lifted her hand to the spot where his

lips had been, very aware of the pounding of her heart and the brightness of the fluorescent lights in the station. Kent started laughing, and Cora dropped her hand.

"Shut up," she said. "Let's eat."

She expected the boys to let the show of affection go and fill their plates with food. No one did.

"So you're dating him?" Charlie asked.

"No," Cora said quickly.

"So he didn't just kiss you?" Jorge said, the first to reach for a plate. He lifted one eyebrow that said, *Yeah, right, girlfriend.*

"It was an interesting weekend," she said.

"Looks like it," Miller said. "Our little Cora has herself a boyfriend."

"He's not—"

"After a single weekend," Charlie added.

"I've heard good things about the Fullers," Max said, and Cora wanted to crawl into a hole and never come out. She could probably leave and they wouldn't notice.

Kent grabbed a slice of the cheesesteak pizza and fell back beside her. "Seriously, Cora. What's going on with you two?"

Cora tucked her hands in the back pockets of her shorts and sighed. "I honestly don't know."

"You kiss him?"

"Technically, he kissed me," she said. "And it was sort of necessary for the ruse at my family's party."

"*Ohhh,* I see. *Necessary.*" Kent took a bite of pizza

and kept one eye on the all-meat pie he liked. "You spent a lot of time with him last week."

"To be able to pull off a fake relationship at the party."

"A fake relationship that looked very real just now."

Fear darted through Cora, and she couldn't swallow properly. Charlie joined them, a plate loaded up with salad and the Alfredo Hawaiian pizza for Cora. He handed it to her, and she nodded at him. Thankfully, no one asked her any other embarrassing questions and the conversation went back to who had the best record in the National League.

Cora ate her food, but the pizza she normally savored tasted like cardboard. By the time she crawled into the bunk way down on the end, away from the men on her squad, her thoughts screamed in her head.

She drew in a breath and thought about the pastor's words from that morning. Believe that you're good enough to make good decisions. And if you ever doubt, ask God.

Cora had relied on one thing since her divorce: her dream to become a hotshot. Every decision she made revolved around that. She knew nothing else. Trusted no other feeling, especially not the soft, sentimental ones that craved another kiss from Brennan Fuller.

She closed her eyes, but sleep didn't claim her instantly. The whisper of Brennan's scent tortured her, the softness of his lips against her cheek, the way he'd become part of her life without her even realizing it.

A smile stretched across her face, and she rolled over.

Lord, she thought, the word clumsy in her mind. *I'm not sure how to talk to you, but I'm wondering if you think it's a good idea for me to continue dating Brennan Fuller?*

She half-expected a bright light to illuminate her bunk. The darkness surrounding her stayed, but her heartbeat slowed and a feeling she hadn't experienced before spread over her like a warm blanket.

She sifted through her vocabulary, trying to give a name to this bliss.

Peace.

Yes, this was peace. She smiled at the idea of pursuing something with Brennan, only a tremor of fear disrupting Cora's comfort.

———

CORA WORKED all day the next day, doing the paperwork her Captain-ship required, as well as putting in the time for the chores she'd assigned herself. She worked out for a couple of hours and wasted the rest of the time on her shift on her phone. By the time she made it over to Brennan's, she'd also spent a good portion of that time texting him.

And when she found him on his front porch, sitting with Sybil panting at his side, a squeal burst from her mouth and she couldn't get her helmet off fast enough. She giggled as she skipped up the walk toward him, glad when he stood to receive her.

"So someone's happy today," he said, sweeping her into his arms. "Good day?"

"It is now."

He looked at her with an edge of wariness in his eye. "Something's different." He backed up. "What is it?"

"Nothing." But Cora's voice strayed into the too-high range. She sat next to the basset hound and scratched behind her ears. "All right, fine. I did what your pastor said to do."

Brennan sat next to her. "And what was that?"

She looked at him, sure he was kidding. "Didn't you hear him yesterday?"

"I was, uh, distracted." He reached for her hand and slipped his fingers between hers. "You sort of smell real nice, and I guess I couldn't use so many senses at once."

Cora blinked, little blips of joy beating through her like a pulse. A laugh flowed from her mouth, and pure happiness filled it, especially when Brennan joined his voice to hers.

"So," she said as she sobered. "He said to believe that we could make good decisions. And if we didn't believe that, to ask God."

"Ah, okay. So you asked God? Or you made your own decision."

"Some of both."

"And what did you decide?"

Cora pulled in a breath, prepared to tell him something real—maybe the first real thing—about herself. "So

I haven't dated in a few years. I mean, I'll go out with men, but nothing serious. I don't want serious."

Brennan's arm flinched, like he was trying to pull it away and keep it in place at the same time. "All right." He sounded wary, guarded, and she didn't really blame him.

"I didn't want serious," she said. "I've been focused on my firefighting. I even came here just to get more rural experience for my application for the hotshot crews."

"Mm hm. You've mentioned that."

She had. Her stomach squirmed, and she wondered if he'd made dinner tonight. "Our relationship was simply going to be one week. The party. Done." And yet, here she sat on this man's front porch, holding his hand. "But I kinda like you, and I asked God if dating you would be okay." She smiled, remembering that delicious feeling of peace. "And I felt good about it."

Brennan's grin was quick and wide. "Wow. That's a lot to live up to."

And she hadn't even told him everything yet. "So yeah. If you're up to it, I think you could be my first boyfriend in four years. My first serious relationship." Her voice cracked on the last word, and she coughed a couple of times.

"Boyfriend. Wow."

"You've already kissed me." She lifted one shoulder in a shrug, and pushed her pigtail off her arm. "If you're not up to it—"

"Oh, I'm up to it."

She smiled at the basset hound, giddiness prancing through her like ponies in a parade.

"Do you want to go to dinner?" he asked. "Are you hungry?"

She nodded. "I am hungry, but I have one more thing to tell you." She lifted her eyes to his, hoping she had the courage to say the necessary words. Hoping against all hope that he wouldn't judge her too harshly.

"The reason I haven't dated seriously—or wanted to date seriously—in four years was because of my divorce."

His eyebrows shot toward his hairline. "You've been married?"

"Yes." The emotion from that event still lingered so close to the surface, and Cora didn't even know it. She swallowed. "His name was Brandt Cowell. We were married for two years. He was a firefighter too."

"What happened?"

Cora wasn't exactly sure, but she couldn't say that. It sounded stupid inside her own head. "He fell out of love with me," she finally said. "I'm not sure when, or why. But he packed everything he owned one day while I was at the station, and when I got home, I found an empty house and a folder of divorce papers on the kitchen counter."

A phantom of that day drifted through her mind's eye, and she lost herself in that depressive darkness where she'd lived for a while after Brandt's departure. "My mother and sister didn't understand it either. That's when I became the black sheep of my family. They all loved Brandt and couldn't understand what I'd done wrong to drive him away."

Brennan remained quiet for several long moments. Then he finally said, "It takes two to tango, right?"

Relief flooded her. "Right."

He inhaled and started to stand. "Thank you for telling me."

"Of course." She joined him and waited while he ushered Sybil back inside the air conditioned house.

"So dinner?"

"One more thing...." She stretched up onto her toes and ran her fingers along the base of his neck, right where his hair ended. He sighed, the breath stuttering out of his body, which drove Cora's desire sky high.

She touched her lips to his at the same time his hands landed on her waist. He kneaded her closer, working his magic on her as he kissed her back. Cora took her time, held on, so she could memorize the taste of him, experience the careful way he seemed to savor her, and let herself have something she hadn't had in a very long time.

Joy.

Peace.

Love?

CHAPTER 8

Brennan went about his business, mowing massive soccer fields and maintaining school grounds during the day, and visiting his grandparents on the weekend. The addition of Cora to his life made him smile every time he woke up, and the evenings and weekends where he could kiss her good-night left him breathless.

She had to work the weekend of Wren's wedding, so he attended that alone. He was actually grateful he didn't have to bring Cora around to meet the entire family. She'd have been overwhelmed in less than a minute. Brennan was, and it was his family.

Gramps and Grams knew about their relationship, and the next time he got together with his brothers, Milt asked, "Hey, whatever happened with you and that firefighter?" He glanced up from the menu, though Brennan was sure his oldest brother already knew what he wanted.

They'd been coming to Ruby's Roost, the ancient café right beside the red brick church, since they were boys. Milt wasn't one to venture past what he already knew he liked—the chicken fried steak—so Brennan suspected his studious attention to the menu was fake.

"We're dating," Brennan said, keeping his eyes on his own menu though he already knew he wanted the fireman's breakfast—and not because of Cora. Ruby's made these fried potatoes that had his mouth watering already.

Pat choked and hastily set down his water glass. "You've got to give me warning," he said. "You're dating her? Like, you go out and hold hands and stuff?" He exchanged a glance with their other unmarried brother, Kyler.

Brennan followed their look, refusing to be embarrassed. So he liked Cora Wesley. So what? "Yes, like we go out and hold hands and...stuff."

Milt leaned back in the booth, the menu forgotten. He wore a big smile and said, "That's great, Brennan."

It was great, and Brennan nodded, glad when Payton came over to take their order. Once the waitress left, Pat leaned forward. "So why didn't you bring her to Wren's wedding?"

"She was on-call and had to be at the station."

"She sleeps there sometimes, right?" Kyler asked. He swept his long hair off his forehead, and Brennan had the sudden urge to drag him down the street to the barber.

"Right."

"And you're okay with that?"

"Why wouldn't I be okay with that?" Brennan narrowed his eyes at Kyler, trying to discern if he knew something Brennan didn't.

"She's the only woman."

"So?"

"So she's sleeping in the same room with all those men."

Brennan hadn't actually given it any thought. He frowned as emotions romped through him. In the end, he said, "I don't think it matters much, Kyler. Honestly."

"All right," he said, lifting one hand in surrender. "If you're not worried about it."

"I'm not."

"Okay."

Milt cleared his throat and reached for the sugar dispenser. While he poured the sweetener into his coffee, he asked, "What about you, Kyler? Are you seeing anyone?"

He laughed, tossing that ridiculous head of hair again. "No, and I'm not looking," he added hastily to the end. "So no karaoke bar. No concerts in the park. I'm doin' just fine on my own."

It was Milt's turn to say, "All right," in a fake, slightly high voice, as if there was no way what Kyler had just said was true.

"You'll have to start looking again at some point," Pat said, his voice at half the volume it had been previously.

"I know, Pat." Kyler glared at him. "I don't need a lecture. I'm doin' just fine."

Brennan kept out of the conversation. Just two years older than Brennan's twenty-nine, Kyler had been his best friend growing up. They were still close, and Brennan knew that Kyler's last girlfriend had been so serious he'd gone to Vernal to look for diamond rings.

When she ghosted him, he cracked. Grew his hair out. Moved to a new house in a somewhat run-down neighborhood. He changed. It had been two years, but Kyler hadn't so much as glanced at a woman in those twenty-four months. And he still had no idea where Katie had gone, where she was now, or why she'd left. All he'd gotten was a note taped to his front door that said, *I'm sorry.*

He met Kyler's eye, the agony there still just as fresh as it had been two years ago. "So Cora wants to be a hotshot," he said, steering the conversation right back to him. "There's a really short window to apply right after Christmas."

Milt went with him, casting one more look in Kyler's direction. "What's a hotshot?"

"Backcountry firefighter," Brennan said. "Sort of. They work for the US Forest Service mostly. Some other organizations, but she wants to get on a crew through the Forest Service. They have crews right here in Utah. They do fire prevention, fight fires obviously, and other stuff to maintain the land."

The conversation continued, and Pat asked Brennan what he'd do if she got selected for a crew somewhere else.

"I don't know," Brennan said, that seed of going to college sprouting in his mind. "Can I tell you guys a secret?" He leaned forward, though he had to immediately lean back as Payton arrived with their food. The conversation stalled as pancakes were passed out, and bottles of ketchup placed on the table.

Once she'd left, Brennan slathered his crispy fried potatoes in ketchup and salt. "You have to promise not to say anything to anyone else. Not Mom and Dad. Not Grams and Gramps. Not any of the girls."

"Like we spend every weekend with Gramps and Grams like you do," Pat said.

"Not your wives either," Brennan said. "They talk to the girls."

"Wow, this must be serious." Milt tucked into his chicken fried steak, obviously not as concerned as he'd sounded.

"I'm thinking about quitting the family business and going back to college."

A loud clanging filled the booth. Brennan's attention shot to Pat, who'd dropped his knife and fork. He blinked at Brennan in pure shock.

"That bad of an idea, huh?" Brennan calmly speared a couple of potatoes, but he couldn't quite put them in his mouth.

"Quitting the family business?" Pat repeated. "Yeah, that's a *huge* idea."

"Pat," Milt said in his warning, older brother voice.

"No one's quit the family business." Pat managed to

pick up his silverware, and he licked the egg yolk from the handle of his knife. "Wow. I just—I had no idea—wow."

"You don't like landscaping?" Kyler asked. He hadn't looked away from Brennan since he'd practically declared he wanted to defect from the Fuller family business. A shimmer of hope glinted in his eyes.

"I like it fine," Brennan said.

"Then why quit?"

"It's not what I want to do."

"What do you want to do?" Milt asked.

"It's stupid." Brennan focused on his food, wishing he'd never brought it up. But if he couldn't talk about it with his brothers, how could he ever approach his parents and have the required conversation?

"I'm sure it's not," Kyler said.

"It's still landscaping," Brennan said, taking courage from the encouragement he found in Kyler's gaze. "But it requires me to go to college. It's called landscape architecture, and you basically work with cities, businesses, universities, places like that, to design campuses, parks, or spaces that are environmentally friendly. It's like landscaping, but on a much bigger scale."

"Not mowing lawns." Kyler looked as interested as Brennan felt about landscape architecture.

"Not mowing lawns," Brennan said. "It's more like deciding where those lawns will be. Preserving green space in big cities. Designing parks for communities. There's all kinds of possibilities in the job market."

"Not in Brush Creek," Pat said, the voice of dissent

and doubt. Or maybe he was the sole voice of reason. Brennan wasn't sure.

"Not in Brush Creek, no," Brennan agreed.

"No one has ever even moved from Brush Creek," he pointed out.

"I know." Brennan sighed. "Doesn't that bother you guys? Did you just feel like, I don't know. You're okay with your jobs? Your lives here?"

"I am," Milt said. "But I don't fault you for wanting something different."

"I'm surprised Dawn hasn't left yet," Kyler said.

Brennan was too. Dawn was the second youngest, and their mother had labeled her the "wild child" of the Fuller family. Silence descended as the brothers ate, and Brennan couldn't help letting the idea of becoming a landscape architect grow, expand, and bloom.

When he got home, he opened his laptop and started researching how to become one, which colleges around the country offered the best programs. He made a list of how much it would cost, how long it would take, and where the best jobs were.

No matter how he looked at it, he couldn't keep his job with A Jack of All Trades and go to school. "Maybe for a year," he said, looking at the list of required classes he'd printed from the Utah State University website. He might be able to do some general education classes online for a couple of semesters.

After that, though, he'd need to be at the university. Physically in classes. And that meant he'd have to quit his job and leave town, something no one in his family had done in three generations.

———

"How many chin ups do you have to do?" Brennan panted, having only done one. He stared at Cora in her tight workout pants and skimpy tank top. Her muscles strained, but her body lifted as if levitated by a magician.

"Six," she grunted.

"How many is that?"

She lowered herself, her arms shaking. Sheer determination coated her face, and she lifted herself once more. "Five."

Brennan admired her for a lot of reasons. She'd come to Brush Creek by herself, number one. She dealt with a toxic family with grace and kindness. She was the hardest worker he'd ever met. Since joining her for her workouts, he'd become very aware of how out of shape he was, despite working ten hours a day on his feet.

Because Cora could run two miles in thirteen minutes. She had to. The hotshots had rigorous physical requirements, and she'd been working for eight months to make sure she could meet them. She'd passed last year, but she hadn't been given a job. While her application remained on file, she had to do the physical tests every year, during the tiny window in the winter.

"Six." She practically flopped to the mat and wiped

the sweat from her forehead. When she looked at him, pure satisfaction beamed from her face.

"I did one," Brennan said, returning her grin. "I think I'm gonna call that good."

She giggled, the pure feminine sound of it lighting Brennan's blood on fire. He turned to survey the rest of her home gym. "What do you do next?" He'd learned that she had a workout routine for every day of the week.

"I'm lifting today," she said, moving to a rack of free weights.

"Oh, well, I'm going to be lifting later, so I'll just watch." He took a seat in the single folding chair in the room.

"Lifting later?" She quirked an eyebrow at him. "What are you going to be lifting later?"

"You know, bags of topsoil. Something like that."

She laughed at him, and Brennan couldn't help himself. He stood and approached her, sweeping one hand around her waist to pull her in for a kiss. He liked the curve of her mouth as he did, liked that she kissed him back, even if it was only for a few seconds.

"Stop distracting me," she said, a flirtatious undercurrent to her voice that meant she wasn't really upset with him. "My test is in four months. I can't be all soft because of you." She pushed on his chest, but he didn't move.

"I like the soft parts of you," he said, holding her close, a prayer in his heart that he wouldn't have to let her go.

She relaxed against him, and Brennan closed his eyes as she settled her cheek against his pulse. He felt dangerously out of control in that moment. Like he could blurt out, "I love you," and she might say it back.

They'd been dating for three months now, and summer was fading into fall in Brush Creek. Combined with all the things she'd told him about herself, he'd learned what a dedicated team member she was. How funny she could be when she was really tired. He adored her positive attitude, and the way she grew quiet when she needed to think about something.

Instead of saying those three little words he felt coiling in his gut, he said, "I've looked into getting a landscape architecture degree."

She bolted away from his body like she'd been shocked. "You have?"

"I've been thinking about it." A lot, actually. His nerves fired on all cylinders. "I mean, if you're going to leave Brush Creek, I was thinking maybe I didn't want to be left behind."

Panic filled her eyes as they widened, and a cold fist smacked Brennan in the chest. "Oh."

She blinked, but that terror didn't leave her eyes. "I— I didn't realize...."

Brennan fell back a couple of steps, his own brand of shock traveling through him, numbing him. "You thought I'd never leave Brush Creek."

Cora finally managed to mask her emotions, which

only threw fuel on Brennan's dormant anger. "Well... yeah."

He gestured between them, throwing off some of the numbness. "So what is this between us?"

"I—I don't know." She replaced the weights she'd picked up and faced him again. "I probably won't get on a crew this year anyway."

"You don't know that."

"I've had my application in for three years. I pass the physical every year. I'm never selected."

"So that was your plan? Date me, kiss me, make me fall in love with you, all while talking about and working toward this grand dream of yours to be on a hotshot crew. But what? You're not going to make it anyway, so it's okay to lead me on?"

Her mouth worked, but no sound came out.

Brennan hated that he'd said "make me fall in love with you." He wasn't even sure if that was how he felt. But he knew he was getting close. "What would you do if you were selected?"

She didn't need to answer. He saw it all on her face.

"That's what I thought." He turned and went back to the chair, bending to pick up his water bottle. He sat down and took a long drink. He had no idea what to say next. Cora obviously didn't either, because she picked up her weights again, turned her back on him, and kept working out.

CHAPTER 9

Cora could barely do a single bicep curl. *Make me fall in love with you* kept rebounding around inside her mind. She'd been asking herself how she felt about Brennan for weeks. She'd been wondering if she should keep chasing the seemingly impossible dream of becoming a hotshot. Maybe she had everything she needed right here in Brush Creek.

She turned back to him. "I was just surprised to hear you'd considered leaving town."

He nodded but said nothing.

"Have you talked with your parents about it?"

"Just Gramps. He says I should do what I think is right."

Cora curled and released, the conversation making it difficult to time her breathing with the motions. "And what's that?"

He lifted those beautiful eyes to hers. "I really like

you, Cora." His voice undid all her defenses, as it always had whenever he finally allowed himself to speak his emotions. She dropped the weight to her side and then to the floor.

She went to him and crouched in front of him, balancing herself with her hands on his knees. "I really like you, too," she whispered. "I don't want to hurt you. I —I honestly don't think I'll get a crew this year."

"Why wouldn't you?"

"I never have before."

"But you'll pass the test," he said, ticking off one finger. "And you have more rural experience this year that you didn't last year. You're the Captain now, and you didn't have that leadership credential last year." He shook his head. "I can't believe you aren't planning on getting chosen."

"I can't believe you think I will." His confidence in her was sexy, and a glow of appreciation seeped through her.

"If you don't believe in yourself, why should anyone else?" He looked at her honestly, his face open and questioning. He leaned forward and touched the tip of his nose to hers. "I believe in you, Cora. I think you're going to get a crew this year, and that's why I'm making plans to leave Brush Creek." He pulled back, the agony in his expression almost too much for her to bear. "Unless you don't want me to leave when you do. Unless—"

"Don't," she said, touching a finger to his lips to silence him. "There's no unless."

"You sure?"

She shook her head, her tumbling emotions making it hard for her to contain them. "I'm not sure of anything," she said. "I wish I had your confidence about the crew. I wish I knew what would happen so we could make real plans. I wish I—" She couldn't finish, because she didn't want him to know the true turmoil inside her. Truth was, she was scared she couldn't fall in love again. That the ability to do so had been taken from her when Brandt left, as if he'd packed it in one of his suitcases when he'd gone.

Brennan curled his fingers around the back of her neck. "You wish what?"

She couldn't tell him, so she hoped a subject change would work. "Have you talked to your parents?"

"No."

So he hadn't made many plans. "Have you applied anywhere?"

"No."

So he'd left everything open as well, just as she had. "You're just thinking about it."

"Yes." He sighed. "I wanted you to know that my options are wide open. If you get a crew in Alaska, if you wanted me to, I'd go with you."

A short burst of laughter came out of her mouth. "I'm not going to Alaska." She straightened and put a few paces of distance between them.

"Why not?" he asked.

"It's freezing there."

The metal chair squeaked as he stood. "So if you got a crew in Alaska, you wouldn't take it?"

She cut a glance at him, and he cocked his head. "You're going to have to say it this time, Cora."

"Yes," she said. "All right? Yes, I'd take it."

His eyes darkened from their normally honey-hazel to more like storm cloud gray. "Which is why I've looked into a dozen colleges and universities from here to Alaska," he said. "But if you don't think this relationship is serious enough for that, I'll stop torturing myself."

"Torturing yourself?"

"Yeah, I'm not the one who needs to do six chin-ups," he said. "Or forty sit-ups in less than a minute." He still looked conflicted, close to upset. But he added, "I'm just here for the view," and chuckled, confusing the heck out of Cora.

She frowned at him. "So you mean the physical torture of working out."

"I mean it all." He turned, picked up his water bottle, and started toward the door. He paused in the doorway that led back into her house, but he didn't face her. "If you tell me you haven't even *thought* about what would happen to us if you got selected for a crew, I don't think we need to keep dating."

Cora's mouth went dry. "Of course I've thought about it."

"And?"

She hated talking to his back, but she said, "I guess I didn't think you'd leave Brush Creek."

"Well, I guess you know different now." With that parting statement, he pushed open the door and left.

Cora stared after him, her chest a swirling tornado. Was it wrong of her to want it all? Want him, and a hotshot crew, and everything else?

She exhaled and moved to the window in the garage she'd converted into a gym. "What would you give up?" she asked her dirty reflection. "Him?" She couldn't imagine a life of happiness without him, and that realization sent a current of electricity through her. When had she fallen for him? When had she passed the point where she'd choose Brennan Fuller over anything else?

Over a hotshot crew? Her brain shrieked at her to know the answer.

Problem was, she didn't know the answer, which only added more dangerous winds to the cyclone sweeping through her soul.

———

ANOTHER MONTH PASSED, and Brennan didn't bring up landscape architecture again. They didn't talk about what would happen if she got assigned to a hotshot crew. He didn't come over and workout with her anymore, but that was about all that had changed.

Well, that, and now she had no idea where she stood with him. No idea if he'd really go with her. No idea if he'd spoken to his parents. She'd met his youngest sister, Berlin. And Wren and her husband. And all of his brothers. He apparently had twin sisters she hadn't met yet, as well as another sister who had a wild streak.

She spent time on Sundays with his grandparents, but she hadn't met his parents yet either. She'd seen the backs of their heads at church, and she knew their names, but that was about it.

"So," she said one evening after coming inside from the autumn rain. He glanced up from where he stood in the kitchen, sprinkling cheese on the sausage and pepper pizza he'd made for her a half dozen times.

"So what?"

"So I think it's time I met your parents." She watched him carefully, unsurprised to see nothing from him. No flinch in the wrist movement as he added more mozzarella. No emotion pouring into his face.

"I don't know," he finally said.

"Why not?"

He dusted his hands and slid the pizza in the oven. "Because," he said with his back turned as he set the timer. "I think we should wait until we know this is serious."

"Brennan." She couldn't help the exasperation that leaked into her tone. "We *are* serious."

He faced her and folded his arms. "Yeah? You think so?"

"You don't? We've been dating exclusively for four months. We see each other every day. You kiss me all the time. I—I've told my friends about you. I—this is serious."

"We have no idea what the future holds."

"Who does?"

He shuttered everything off, the way he'd been doing since their argument in her gym. "I'd like to wait until we know about your crew."

"That's months away."

He softened and came around the counter to embrace her. "I know it is, and I hate that. I wish we knew, so we could make plans, get everything out in the open."

"They know you're dating someone."

"Yes, they do. And they've asked to meet you too."

"What?" She pushed back so she could see his face. "Brennan, come on. This is just you being...I don't know what."

"Scared to get hurt," he blurted. "That's what this is." He stepped back, exhaled out his frustration, and ran his hand up the back of his neck. She'd seen him do it loads of times when he had a lot on his mind, or when he was flustered as he was now.

Cora stared at him as her phone vibrated in her back pocket. Maybe being with him was too hard. Maybe it wasn't meant to be. Maybe she would never be able to reassure him that she wanted to be with him, that she could love him.

The call ended, and something pricked her mind. She pulled her device out and looked at it, seeing a number she didn't recognize.

"Who was it?" he asked, as if that was what mattered right now.

"I don't know." The icon to indicate she had a new voicemail appeared in the top menu, and she swiped down to dial in.

"You have one new message and two saved messages. New message: Hi, this is Gaylan Vespario from the United States Forest Service. I'm calling for Cora Wesley. There's some extreme fire danger in the Los Padres National Forest, and we're hiring temporary hotshots for the next four months. Your name popped up, and I'm wondering if you'd be available to come to California, pretty much immediately."

He continued talking, but Cora's arm didn't have the strength to hold her phone up. It dropped to the floor with a deafening, destructive clatter as more emotions than Cora could contain rose through her like a giant tidal wave.

Brennan approached; his mouth moved; she couldn't hear him. She felt removed from everyone and everything, with only a roaring white noise in her ears.

Only when he touched her face did she jolt back to reality. "You're crying," he said. "What's wrong?" He cradled her face in his hands, and Cora knew in that moment that she'd fallen in love with him. She also knew that she'd leave immediately—right now if she had to— for California.

"They have a hotshot job in California," she whispered. "I have to go." She pulled out of his warm hands and retrieved her phone before sprinting for the exit.

"Cora!" he called. "Wait!"

She didn't wait. She couldn't. She flung her leg over her motorcycle and revved the engine before tearing down the street. When she was safely away from Brennan, she'd call the Forest Service back. She'd worked her whole adult life for this opportunity, and she couldn't let her soft feelings for a man she'd met four months ago change her decision.

Right? she prayed as she finally slowed her bike and pulled over. She peered up into the cold sky, the stars twinkling down on her. "Right, Lord?"

She hoped for that exhilarating and comforting peace she'd felt before.

She felt nothing.

CHAPTER 10

___

When Brennan got stressed, he loaded Sybil into his pickup and drove. So after Cora had practically sprinted from his house, he found himself behind the wheel as darkness took over the day.

They have a hotshot job in California.

His fingers tightened on the steering wheel. Of course they had a firefighting job in California. It seemed like the whole state was on fire right now.

"You wanted her to get this opportunity," he told himself, his words quickly getting swallowed by the silence.

And he did. Just not right now. He hadn't spent any more time researching colleges and landscape architecture degrees since their mini-argument a month ago. He felt fully committed to making sure they could be together no matter what happened. Cora...not so much.

At least that was the vibe he'd picked up over the past few weeks. So no, he did not want her to meet his parents. Didn't want to get the whole family ruffled up over a woman who would probably forget about him when the hotshot call came.

"And that's exactly what just happened." He ground his teeth together, wishing he wasn't quite so easy to leave behind. Wasn't so darn forgettable.

So while his first instinct had been to chase her tail-lights into the night, he wouldn't. Couldn't. She'd said, "I have to go," and he agreed with her. She did have to go do this. It was everything she'd worked for and wanted for three years.

He just wished she had room in her dreams for him.

And so he drove, his mind churning through emotions, and his brain spitting out new feelings that needed to be analyzed. In the end, he wound up exactly where he'd known he would: Gramps's driveway.

It wasn't as late as it felt, but he still approached the front door slowly. Pops barked, and a low sound followed, which meant Gramps was still up. Brennan knocked and entered a moment later with, "It's just me, Gramps."

"Brennan, come on in." He patted Pops and added, "See, Popsy? It's just Brennan."

Pops's tongue hung out of his mouth and his tail went whap, whap, whap against the armrest while he stood with his paws on the back of the couch.

"Yep," Brennan said, wishing the dog's enthusiasm

could rub off on him. "Just me." He exhaled as he sat on the couch opposite of Gramps, leaning back and closing his eyes. This seemed like a great place to stay for the night, and he wondered if he could sneak downstairs to the bedroom where he and his brothers used to sleep when they stayed over.

"What's got your knickers all twisted?"

Brennan wanted to smile, but his face couldn't quite complete the action. Gramps knew about Cora, and he might even have some really great advice. But Brennan's brain was simply too full tonight.

"Nothin'," he said. "Just wanted to come see you."

"Humph." Gramps picked up the remote and pointed it at the TV. "There's nothing on. Bad news and that reality TV I don't like."

"What about those fixer upper shows you like?" Gramps had been a master carpenter when he worked for A Jack of All Trades, and Brennan had learned a few skills with a hammer from him.

"Oh, I've seen 'em all." He jabbed at the buttons and the TV turned off. "Want some coffee?"

"Yeah, sure." Brennan followed him into the kitchen, where the old man hobbled around to get the coffee made. "Where's Cora tonight?"

Brennan wiped his hands down his face. "I reckon she's on her way to California." Surely she couldn't be already. She'd left his place an hour ago, and she had her own house and animals to take care of. Surely she couldn't take two cats and a dog with her into the fiery fray.

No, she probably wouldn't leave until morning. Maybe later. She did have a job at the fire station to take care of too. She couldn't just cut and run from that. She'd wanted to be a hotshot, sure, but she wasn't one to burn bridges.

"California?" Gramps yelled as if he'd never heard of the place. "Why would she go there?"

"She got that hotshot job she's been talking about," Brennan said.

"Oh." Gramps got out the sugar bowl and two mugs, making a big racket as he did. Brennan had seen behavior like this before—Gramps made noise when he didn't want to have a conversation. Brennan's dad did the same thing.

But the coffee brewed, and there wasn't much to be done but sit and sip after that. "I'm sorry," he said. "Is that it?"

"Feels like it," Brennan said.

"I didn't ask how you feel," Gramps said, a bit gruff around the edges. "I asked if that was it."

"I don't know." Brennan added more sugar to his coffee, as Gramps really liked the dark roast and it was very bitter. "We hadn't worked out what to do if she got a hotshot job. The assignments weren't supposed to come through until February. She wasn't even going to take her physical until the end of the year."

He felt like he'd been robbed. Robbed of four more months with her. Robbed of the time he needed to figure out where she'd be, and how he could go with her, and if she even wanted any of that.

His breath hitched, and he took another long sip of the coffee, glad it was a little bitter still. It tasted like he felt.

"So what are you going to do?"

"Let it lie," he said. "She'll need a few days to get settled, and then...then, I don't know." Calling and begging sounded pathetic, though it was what he wanted to do. He'd only told his brothers about the landscape architecture, and that hadn't exactly gone over well. He could still see Pat's incredulity and hear the disbelief in his voice.

Gramps nodded, though Brennan couldn't remember what he'd have said for his grandfather to agree with. "Do you know how Grams and I met?"

"Yeah, sure," Brennan said. "You stalked her after the strawberry festival and stopped by her house every day after work until she agreed to go out with you." The smile he'd tried for earlier finally came to his mouth.

"Oh." Gramps blustered out the word. "I did not stalk her."

Brennan chuckled. "I know, Gramps."

"I was persistent though. I thought she was a stunning woman, and I didn't give up until I got what I wanted."

Brennan wasn't so sure that would still work in this

day and age, but it was a nice sentiment. "How did you win her over?"

"With my charm and good looks, of course!" He pounded one fist on the countertop, making the coffee in his mug tremble. He laughed, a big hearty laugh that told Brennan he'd lived a happy and full life.

The thought of leaving Gramps and Grams hit him square in the chest. He'd honestly never considered that he'd be leaving his two favorite people behind if he chose to follow Cora wherever her crew went.

It wasn't a choice at all. He loved his grandparents, but he didn't need to see them every day. He didn't get fulfillment from making them laugh. His heartrate didn't get worked up when they walked in the room. They didn't make him want to be a better man.

Cora did all of that, and yes, Brennan would follow her wherever she went.

"I have to go," he said, using the same words Cora had.

"Gonna go talk to Cora, right," Gramps said.

"Can I leave Sybil here?" Brennan called as he entered the living room and found Sybil and Pops passed out on the couch together.

"Sure thing," Gramps yelled from the other room. Brennan yanked open the front door and hurried through it. He had no idea what to say to Cora, or how to express his feelings, as deep as they were.

He just knew she couldn't leave town without him laying all the cards on the table.

"Then we'll see if she can forget me," he muttered to himself as he leapt behind the wheel of his pickup.

TWO HOURS LATER, Brennan had to admit defeat. Cora hadn't been home when he'd arrived. Her windows still sat in darkness, and maybe Brennan had cupped his hands around his eyes to peer inside her living room window. Her cats were gone. And that huge great Dane too. Pippa barked like a psychopath whenever anyone got too close to the door, so he should've known as soon as he knocked that Cora wasn't home.

He'd settled on the steps to wait, thinking maybe she was over at the station, taking care of things. Her motorcycle wasn't in the driveway, and no way she could pack everything she needed for a twelve-hour drive to California in a backpack.

She had a sedan she used in the winter, but it sat way back in the driveway where it had been all summer.

When the clock ticked to eleven, Brennan stood from his position on her front porch. Feeling very much like the stalker he'd just accused Gramps of being, he ducked his head and went on home.

The following morning, he headed over to her house before the sun had fully lit the sky. She must not have slept at all, because the bike sat on the sidewalk and the sedan was gone.

Brennan got out of his truck anyway, the mood in

the air somber. The house almost felt like it had been abandoned, though that made so sense. His heart kicked around in his chest, unhappy at not being able to say good-bye to Cora properly. Frustrated that she'd left without giving them a chance to have a conversation. Worried that it would never get to see Cora again.

A piece of paper flapped in the wind, lifting off the shiny red helmet where she'd taped it. He walked toward it slowly, almost wanting to leave it right where it was, forget about her, and go about his mowing and raking for the day. It would snow soon in these hills, and all the leaves had to be up before that happened.

But he kept on, pulling his jacket tighter around him as he reached the note. She had his phone number. She could text him anything that was time-sensitive if he chose not to read this memo she'd left behind.

He wasn't sure how long he stood there staring at it. Long enough for his nose to get cold and his fingers to ache from the way he held them in fists inside his pockets.

Finally, he plucked it from the helmet and opened it.

BRENNAN,

I'm sorry I had to leave town like this. I hope you'll be able to forgive me one day. I've got my men coming over to box everything up and put it in storage. I gave my cats and Pip to Kent. If you want them, they're yours. In fact, anything in the house you want, you can have.

. . .

He snorted. Like he wanted two shorthaired cats and a dog the size of a pony. He looked up into the sky. "I want *her*," he whispered to the clouds, to God. "How do I get her?"

A rain drop fell, his only answer. He turned and went back to the truck, still reading.

I sold my motorcycle to Sergio Reyes. He said he'd come get it later today. The keys are in the seat. I don't know why I'm telling you this. You're not going to be around anyway.

He could almost imagine her sighing at this point, her sign that she was about to wrap it up. Sure enough, there was only one line left in the letter, and it said, *Once I get my bearings, I'll call you.*

Cora

Brennan crumpled the letter in his fist and tossed the ball of paper to the floor on the passenger side of the truck. He didn't want anything from her house. He didn't want her pets. And he certainly didn't want to wait an undetermined amount of time before hearing from her.

But her meaning had been clear: *Wait for me.*

Brennan wasn't sure if he could. Well, of course he *could*. He wasn't sure he *wanted* to. Fury pounded behind his eyes that she'd even asked him to, and red was all he could see as he drove away from her house.

CHAPTER 11

A week had passed since Cora had snuck out of Utah like a thief in the night. Her back ached, and she rolled over on the tiny cot she carried tied to her pack. The air was scented with ash and fire, as usual.

She'd woken before dawn, as usual. Every inch of her skin felt tight like a drum, and dry dry dry. No amount of lotion could soothe the windswept, fire-singed, sunburned flesh on her neck and face.

"You up?"

She turned toward Davy's low whisper and groaned as she stretched. "Yep. Why are you up?"

He drew something in the dirt where he crouched. "Couldn't sleep." He pointed to the orange glow on the horizon. "It's not slowing down." He was a few years older than her, and had been on a hotshot crew in New

Mexico for a year before coming to California to help with the fires.

There were over eight thousand additional firefighters and hotshots currently in the state, all of them trying to tame the difficult flames before they destroyed more homes, ruined more land, killed more animals. The crews attempted to get ahead of the blaze and burn out its fuel. Anything to get this fire under control.

"Where's Jaxon?"

"He was on the first watch, so he's still asleep." Davy yawned. "Your morning crew is starting to stir on the other side of camp."

She nodded and stood, not wanting to be the last of her crew to be up and ready for the day. She'd been assigned to the Del Rosa Hotshots Crew when three of it's members had been life-flighted out of the area due to a wind kicking up and throwing the flames in their faces, all in under three seconds.

She'd learned quickly that fire was no joke, especially out here, where there were limited medical supplies, limited ways to communicate, and a Mother Nature that didn't care if you thought you were invincible.

Cora certainly didn't think she was infallible, and she glanced up as the now-familiar sound of a fire helicopter came closer. The pilots worked day and night, keeping their crafts running and fueled, flying out to the front lines, and dropping buckets of fire retardant and water. Sometimes they even dropped supplies for the hotshots, but Cora hadn't seen that for herself yet.

She pulled on her too-big boots and clomped clumsily over to her crew. She was the only female hotshot on the Del Rosa crew, and nothing they'd given her fit well. Everything was too big, too long, too bulky. For the first time in her life, she was glad for her boxy shoulders, as they at least held her coat in place while she used a chainsaw to cut back overgrowth that would burn in the blink of an eye.

Her job—along with the rest of her crew—was to clear the way for the fire. Which meant they were in the direct path of the flames, and they worked ahead to try to eliminate all the fuel the fire needed to continue.

She wore heavy-duty fire clothing for sixteen hours a day under the suffocating California sun. She carried a fifty-pound pack with all her clothes, toiletries, fire retardant, first aid kit, emergency supplies, and more. Attached to that, she had her cot, an axe, and as much water as she could carry.

In her hands, she wielded a chainsaw, a skill she'd never thought she'd need as much as she had when she'd first come to California. Some of her crew came behind and cleared the debris she created, and behind them came the soakers. They dumped water and fire retardant on the cleared areas, hoping that when the flames reached them, they'd die.

"We've got this fire eighty percent contained," Gil said as she approached. "A couple more days, guys, and we could have it out."

A couple more days. That sounded fantastic to Cora.

She needed a hot shower and a soft bed. Shoes that fit. And a chance to call Brennan.

She hadn't spoken to him once in the past eight days, something that ate at her soul and made her heart writhe in her chest uncomfortably. But she didn't even have her cell phone out here. She'd been given a crew radio, and that was how they kept in touch if things went south. She was never supposed to be alone anyway, so having a personal cell phone was frivolous.

"Cora, you're on soaking today." Gil met her eye and waited for her to nod. Passing the heavy chainsaw to someone else for a day would be a relief, though she'd been grateful for the dozens of pushups she'd inflicted upon herself once she'd gotten out here. She couldn't believe she'd only been removed from civilization for five days. It felt like a lot longer than that.

One day to drive, she chanted as she suited up. One day to complete her physical and get her assignment. One day to get transported to her crew base. On the fourth day after leaving Utah, she'd been on the front lines of the fire, doing exactly what she'd dreamt of doing.

She reminded herself that she *wanted* to be out here in California's wilderness. Even with the baggy pants and the floppy gloves. Even with the huge packs and heavy chainsaws. Even with the acrid scent of smoke and death all around her.

Thank you, she sent toward the awakening sky. She learned the value of prayer every day she was out here, and she didn't want to miss a day of thanking the Lord for the opportunity to be exactly where she was.

Her thoughts lingered on the man she'd left behind, and she added *Please help him to forgive me*, to her prayer. Then she stuck her hard hat on her head, picked up a bucket of fire retardant and followed her crew toward the untamed wilderness they needed to clear that day.

———

Cora got exactly twenty-four hours of rest before her next assignment came in. The Del Rosa crew had helped immensely in the Gibbons Fire, but another blaze loomed too close to a neighborhood in the Angeles National Forest. She and her nineteen crew members were shipping out in an hour, and Cora stared at her phone, trying to get up the courage to send a text to Brennan.

Kent had texted to say he'd never come to get her pets. Cora had thought he would, and the fact that he hadn't sent a very clear message to her.

Sergio had texted to say he'd gotten the bike without a problem. Charlie had texted to say the house was boxed and stored and back up for rent.

Feeling officially homeless, because she was, she hung her head and let her phone drop to the bed beside her. The US Forest Service had put her up in the Del Rosa Hotshots facilities, but a single room with a twin bed was hardly paradise. Still, it was a roof and it wasn't on fire. There was running water and hot food and good company.

But there wasn't Brennan. There wasn't even the hope of Brennan. And she hated that.

"Let's go, Wesley," Gil barked, rapping his knuckles on her open door as he passed by in the hallway.

She stood, her opportunity to make contact with Brennan nearly over. Even if she texted now, she'd have ten minutes to get a response. It was the middle of the day, and he could be out working on any number of things.

Men's voices filtered down the hall to her, urging her to hurry up or she'd be left holding her pack on her lap during the transport. Making a quick decision, and seizing the opportunities given to her, she tapped out a message to Brennan.

Back from my first fire. It was insane. Can't wait to tell you all about it. Shipping out to the next location. It's the Thompson Creek Fire, if you want to follow it on the news. Won't have my phone.

She stared at the words, wondering if she could put how she really felt. Wondering if it would be too unfair to tell him she loved him and missed him.

"Wesley!" Gil yelled.

Her fingers flew and she only added two more words before jamming her thumb on the SEND button and stuffing her phone in her back pocket.

Miss you.

She wasn't sure if it would make Brennan smile or make him want to smash something. Guilt ate away at her, but she wasn't good enough friends with anyone on the crew to pour her history out and ask their advice.

She managed to shove her pack into a space two sizes too small for it before she climbed on the bus. Ignoring Gil's death glare, she found a seat near the middle and turned her attention out the window.

With her phone clutched in her hand so she could feel it when it vibrated, she watched the city go by, clouded with smoke from the Thompson Creek Fire. The crew arrived seemingly in the blink of an eye, and Cora powered down her phone and stuck it in an outside pocket on her pack.

Brennan hadn't responded, and Cora's heart settled in her overly large boots as she set about hauling all her equipment toward the shelters.

Have I done the wrong thing? she wondered. She expected to be happier as a hotshot, but one thing was for certain—she wasn't happier here than she had been in Utah.

"Heads up!" someone called at the same time another man yelled, "Watch out!"

Cora flinched, shrinking into herself at the same time she tried to look up and find whatever had everyone concerned.

The sky held an eerie shade of dark green, but Cora couldn't see anything else. Someone else yelled, and she threw her hands up to protect her head. Time stilled, and something rushed through the air.

She turned just in time to see the flaming debris, but she couldn't get out of the way fast enough. The piece of wood hit her square in the face, and pain exploded up her nose and down her throat.

She gasped and grunted and gagged all in the same breath, and her knees hit the dirt. Everything spun, and she closed her eyes to keep from throwing up. The sound of footsteps raced toward her, along with men calling to one another.

"Cora," someone said and it echoed endlessly in her head. *Cora, Cora, Cora.*

"Look at me, Cora."

She recognized the voice as Gil's, but she couldn't make her eyes obey. They were shut and they wanted to stay that way.

"She's burnt," she heard Gil say. "Get the first aid kit. Call the med unit. They'll have to come get her. We're going out on the fireline in twenty minutes."

No, Cora screamed inside her own head. She didn't want to be left behind. She wanted to be on the fireline in twenty minutes. She tried to sit up. Tried to tell Gil she was fine. But the cool darkness she floated in took her further and further from her senses, until all that remained was nothingness.

CHAPTER 12

Missing was not a strong enough verb for Brennan's agony over Cora's departure. She'd been gone for eleven days before he got a message from her. And curse his luck, he'd been on the riding mower for hours and thus, hadn't heard the chime nor felt the buzz.

Back from my first fire. It was insane. Can't wait to tell you all about it. Shipping out to the next location. It's the Thompson Creek Fire, if you want to follow it on the news. Won't have my phone. Miss you.

"Miss you," he repeated to himself, wondering how in the world he could adequately convey how he felt about her through a text. With the heater blowing on his fingers, he managed to get them working, but he didn't send a text to Cora. She wouldn't get it anyway.

No, he swiped and tapped until his phone called his

father. "Hey, Bren," he said, his voice as cheerful and chipper as ever.

"Hey, Dad." Brennan stared out the windshield at the huge field to the west of the recreation center. It was the last time he'd have to mow it this season, and he was grateful for that.

Actually, it might have just been the last time he mowed that field, period.

"What's up, bud?"

Brennan heard the whir of a saw in the background. "Dad, do you have time to talk?"

"Yeah, sure." The saw sound faded, and Brennan decided to just blurt everything out.

"I don't want to work for A Jack of All Trades anymore," he said, his voice scratching against his throat. "I want to go to college and get a degree in landscape architecture."

The silence on the other end of the line made Brennan's lungs pinch.

"Dad? You still there?"

"Yeah."

"Where are you? Maybe I should come over and we can talk."

"I'm out at the Robinson build. I should be done here in about an hour. I'll call Mom and see if she wants to cook or go out. Sound good?"

"Yeah, that sounds good."

"I'll let you know." His father hung up, leaving Brennan just as unsettled as he had been before. He was done for the day, so he headed home and spent the time until dinner researching colleges in California that offered the landscape architecture degree. Frustration coiled through him as his list of links swelled.

He had no idea where in California Cora would even be. Sure, she was out in the Thompson Creek Fire right now, but where would she be housed? Where would she live?

Brennan didn't know, but he needed to feel like he was doing something, so he compiled his list and saved it before heading across the river and over to his parents' house.

The scent of smoked sausage filled the air outside the front door, and Brennan took a moment to appreciate all he had in his life. He'd had a great childhood. Lots of siblings to play with, and doting grandparents, and a backyard that was as big as a park. He'd never wondered if he'd have enough money or not, and he'd never gone without something he wanted.

Until now. Until Cora.

Buoyed up by his decision, he pushed into the house to find his mom singing in the kitchen the way she normally did when she'd had a great day. Of course, she thought any day where she got to cook was amazing.

His dad's lower voice joined his mom's, and Brennan leaned against the corner of the wall to watch them work together to finish the meal. They displayed such love for each other. Sure, he knew they didn't always get along, but he could also plainly see how well they fit together.

The song ended, and he applauded, startling them both. "There he is," his mom said, rushing forward, her carefree singing in the past now. She embraced Brennan and trailed her fingernails down the side of his face. "You want to quit?"

"Let's eat first," his dad said, casting an unreadable look at Brennan. He dished up a platter of rice and beans and set it on the table with the rest of the soft shell taco ingredients.

Brennan sat in Berlin's chair and started assembling a burrito. "So I'm in love with Cora Wesley, and she just got a job as a hotshot in California. I want to go be with her."

His mother's smile couldn't have been any wider. "In love with her? That's wonderful, sweetheart." She patted his hand like he was a five-year-old and had just said something cute.

"What about this landscape architecture?" his dad asked.

"It's something I've always been interested in," Brennan said. "But college never seemed to be an option for me, and I didn't realize until recently how much I want to go. Do something on my own." He finished rolling his burrito and glanced at his dad. "Not that I'm not grateful for the job, the work, all of it. It's been great. I just...." He searched for the right words and couldn't quite find them.

"You just want something different," his dad said.

"Yes and no," Brennan said. "I don't really want to

leave Brush Creek. But what I want to do means I can't stay here."

"We'll be short-staffed without you," his dad said. "You take care of two huge contracts."

"I know." Brennan nodded and lifted his burrito to his mouth. After taking a huge bite to give himself time to think, he weighed some options. He swallowed and said, "You could hire someone, Dad. There are plenty of men who would love to work for you."

"It's a family business." His father waved Brennan's suggestion away like he was swatting a fly.

"I think Brennan should go," his mom said quietly, bringing Dad's neck around in whiplash-like fashion.

"Quincey."

"He should follow his heart." She beamed at Brennan again. "He's in love with her, and her job is taking her somewhere else." She lifted her chin and looked right into his father's eyes. "I think he should be able to go if he needs to. No guilt."

"I can stay and help whoever you hire," Brennan said. "I can wait another month before I go." College classes had already started for the fall anyway. He wouldn't be able to start until January, so he had almost two months to spare.

His father's shoulders deflated and he nodded. "All right. I'll start asking around tomorrow."

Brennan couldn't help the whoop that came from him. "Thanks, Dad." He'd just finished his burrito when his phone rang. His heart catapulted to the back of his throat, anticipating that it could be Cora.

Don't be dumb, he told himself. She'd said she wouldn't have her phone.

The number on the screen was a California number, and something inside him urged him to take the call. He stood from the table and said, "Excuse me," as he swiped to open the call. "Hello?"

"Hello, this is Doctor Simon Wilson. I'm a general care physician at the USC Verdugo Hills Hospital in Glendale, California. A woman named Cora Wesley was brought in and you're the emergency contact in her phone. To whom am I speaking?"

Brennan's heart flopped around inside his chest like a sputtering balloon. "Brennan Fuller," he said.

"Are you married to Miss Wesley?"

"No, sir."

"Brother?"

"I'm her boyfriend," he said. "She has family in Vernal."

"If you aren't her relations, I can't give you personal information, but perhaps you could pass a message onto the family. We're swamped with the fire so close, and short-staffed...."

"Of course," Brennan blurted. "I can pass on a message."

"Great." The relief in Doctor Wilson's voice was palpable. "She was brought in by one of the hotshot medical crews. She's been hit with a blunt, burning object, and she's here in the hospital, unconscious. We need someone here who can make decisions on her behalf."

Brennan could barely think. No, he couldn't make decisions on her behalf. But he needed to get to California as fast as possible.

"I'll call her mother," he managed to rasp out of his dry throat. "Thank you for calling."

He turned back to the kitchen, where his parents sat watching him. "Cora's been hurt." He strode to the counter, where he'd tossed his wallet. "I'm going to California."

"What?" His mother stood, her chair scraping the tile. "Right now?"

"Right now," he said. "I'll stop at home and pack a few things. Get a ticket. Call her mom...." He listed the things he needed to do, then mentally went over it again.

He left his parents in their kitchen and drove ten over the speed limit back to his house. Within a half an hour, he'd packed and booked an airplane ticket out of Salt Lake for the following morning. As he set his truck west to make the four-hour drive to the airport, he realized he didn't have her mother's number. Or Helene's. Or Cora's father's. He couldn't make medical decisions for her, and they'd want to know about her injury.

His stomach twisted at the very thought of making medical decisions. That had to be some serious stuff, and he wondered what had hit Cora.

"Lord," he said out loud. "Please." His throat tightened, but he pushed on. "I'm begging you. Protect her. Help her heal. Bless her to not sustain anything too serious from this injury."

A sense of calmness entered him, eradicating his half-pieced together thoughts. He picked up his phone and said, "Call Wren Fuller," realizing he needed to change his sister's last name now that she'd married Tate.

"Hey," she said. "What's up, you?"

"I can't really explain everything right now," he said in a rush as he approached the top of the hill. There was a dead spot for cell reception on the other side. "But I need you to get a couple of phone numbers for me."

"I can do that. Who?"

He searched his brain for Cora's parent's names. "Laura Wesley," he said. "Or Chris Wesley. They live in Vernal."

"I'll text you the numbers. Where are you?"

"On my way to get Cora back," he said, a very final note of determination in his voice.

CHAPTER 13

A very odd noise existed inside Cora's mind. It was steady, and strong, and annoying. She tried to open her eyes, tried to figure out where she was. Her eyelids seemed sewn shut as a new sound registered in her ears.

A voice.

A voice she knew.

And pressure on her fingers. She squeezed back, and the voice yelped. The annoying, steady sound increased, and she knew what it was: a heart monitor.

Monitoring her heart.

Everything returned to her memory in a whoosh of sound, light, and pain. Her eyes flew open, searching for the man the voice belonged to.

"Brennan," she said, her throat rusty and making his name sound like a frog had spoken it.

"Hey, baby." He bent over her, both of his hands

clasping hers. "There you are." He reached up and brushed her hair off her forehead.

"What—?" She tried to sit up, but her head felt woozy and soft. "Whoa."

"Don't move," he said. "Your mom's getting the nurse."

Her mom. The pounding in Cora's head only intensified. Not only would she have to endure snide remarks about her life, but she'd surely get a verbal berating on her career choice too.

The door in the corner opened and two nurses and her mother came through it. "Hello, Cora," one woman said as she looked at the heart monitor and back to Cora's face. "I'm Betsy. How are you feeling?"

"My head hurts."

"I bet it does." Betsy nodded to the other woman, who left.

"Do you remember what happened?"

Cora sighed, the flaming debris flying at her all over again. "Yeah."

"Well, you broke your nose," Betsy said. "And you've got a skull fracture along your right eyebrow there. There's not a whole lot we can do about either of those but make you comfortable until they heal."

The other nurse returned, and Betsy swiveled toward her. "So Dina's got another thousand of ibuprofen, and we'll let the doctor know you're awake."

"What about my crew?" she asked.

Betsy's face blanked, and she glanced at Brennan. "Crew?"

"I'll tell her," Brennan said, flashing the nurse a brilliant smile that made Cora wonder how on earth she thought she could leave him behind in Brush Creek. And for what? To saw through logs, haul off undergrowth, and get hit in the face when the fire started spitting out debris?

She waited until Betsy and Dina left, then she blurted, "I'm so sorry, Brennan."

He sat in the chair he'd been in earlier and smiled. "It's fine."

"How did you know?"

"Apparently, I'm your emergency contact in your phone. The doctor here called me after the medical team from the Forest Service brought you in."

Cora let her head fall back to the pillow, the worst edge of pain already easing from the drugs Dina had put right into her veins. Tears gathered in her eyes, but she didn't want to let them fall. She wouldn't be weak, not now, not when she'd come this far.

"I think you said you couldn't wait to tell me all about your first fire." He put both his hands around hers again and lifted her wrist to his lips.

She marveled at him. At the handsome lines in his face. His easy forgiveness. His solid, silent strength.

"I love you," she whispered.

Surprise danced across his face, melting into pure

adoration. "I love you, too, Cora." He tipped forward, his lips touching hers for the briefest of moments.

Her mom cleared her throat and said, "I'll go get you...something to drink." She high-tailed it out of the room, the kindest thing Cora thought she'd ever done for her.

Cora looked back at Brennan, that same brilliant tether that had locked them together at the karaoke bar still present. Stronger. Better. She hoped their relationship would always be this exciting, and new, and wonderful.

"So tell me about the fire."

She shook her head. "It was a fire. We need to talk about what we're going to do now."

He quirked one eyebrow and gave her half a smile. "What we're going to do now is get married."

Cora choked, sending the heart monitor into a frenzy. Brennan chuckled. "I mean, not right away, of course. But I've already talked to my parents, and I'm going to be moving to California by Christmas." He bent toward her again, his eyes closing as he touched his forehead to hers.

A tiny slice of pain radiated behind her right eye, but he was soft and gentle in his touch, and the ache settled into nothing. "When I met you that first time, I knew we'd be together. I knew I'd follow you wherever you went. I knew I'd stay with you for a long time."

"You did?" Cora's voice squeaked and those darn tears squeezed out of her closed eyes.

"I sure did." He swept his lips behind her ear and whispered, "I'm in love with you, and I want to marry you, and I'm going to go to school while you fight fires. How does that sound?"

"Amazing," she breathed.

"So, where should I be looking for housing and a place to go to school?"

She opened her eyes, and he drew back. "I don't know."

"You don't know? Where do you live?"

"I didn't have to get a place. I stayed in the hotshots barracks and then we were out in the wilderness. I was back for one day—again in the barracks—and then we were on our way to the Thompson Creek Fire."

He nodded, seemingly undeterred. "Do you think you'll be able to stay on your crew?"

She felt helpless and ridiculous when she said, "I have no idea."

Brennan searched her face as if looking for something that would tell him what to do. He finally said, "All right. Well, here's what I'm going to do. You're on the Del Rosa Crew right now, right?"

"Yes."

"They're located here in Southern California. I'm going to find somewhere to live that's very close to the university where I'll be going, and we can work from there."

Cora had no idea what to say. She knew he needed a place to live. Needed something to do that felt worthwhile to him. Needed a plan of action so he could *do something*. And since she didn't have any of those things to give him, she smiled. "I love you."

He grinned. "I kinda like you too."

"I'll start praying I get on the Del Rosa Crew permanently," she said.

"I'll do that too." He stood, releasing her hands and letting a sigh sift through his lips. "I'll go rescue your mom from the vending machine. I'm sure she wants to talk to you."

Cora groaned, which made Brennan laugh somehow. "Don't worry. She's been really nice while we've been here together."

"How long have you guys been here?"

"Just a few hours," he said. "You've only been asleep for, oh, sixteen hours or so." He lifted his hand in a wave and disappeared through the doorway.

Cora sat very still, trying to work things out in her head. Brush Creek was a healthy four-hour drive to the airport. He and her mother must've driven for most of the night and boarded the first plane to Los Angeles to be by her bedside when she woke up.

A rush of appreciation filled her, and those pesky tears pricked at her again. When her mom opened the door and peered cautiously inside, Cora let them fall. Her mother rushed forward and said, "Oh, don't cry, sweetheart. Everything's going to be okay."

———

CORA GOT out of the hospital the next day. She rejoined her crew in the Angeles National Forest with a bandage on her nose, which Gil said looked "hard-core" and "tough." He put her right to work, and this time, their crew was on the tail end of the fire.

The mask she'd been given was, of course, too big, and she sucked in to keep it flush against her face. The backend of a fire was filled with smoke and the last thing she needed was another trip to the hospital.

She worked with a different purpose now. Number one, her job was to find any remaining hotspots and put them out completely. Number two, she needed to find out what her future with this crew would be. She owed it to Brennan to have more answers for him than she'd had in the hospital.

He'd returned to Utah last night, along with her mother. Their visit, though a bit embarrassing, had added a glow to her life that Cora hadn't felt in years. She prayed that she would be good enough to earn a permanent spot on the Del Rosa Crew, and that she could have everything she wanted. The job. The man. The family.

The Thompson Creek Fire was contained the next day, and the crew returned to their work camp in San Bernardino. After showering and plugging in her phone, she got up the courage to go talk to Gil, the Superintendent of the Crew.

"Hey, can I steal you for a sec?" she asked when she found him in the main room with several other men.

"Sure thing." The bear of a man got up and followed

her outside, which was blessedly smoke-free. "How's the face?"

"It's fine," she said, reaching up to touch her eyebrow. If she ran her fingers along it, she could feel an indentation where her skull had been chipped. "Doesn't hurt." She drew in a deep breath. "Thanks for making sure the burns wouldn't be scarring on my face."

"Yeah, of course. If there's one thing I know how to treat, it's a burn. Yours was mild. Nothing to worry about." His blue eyes pierced her, almost like he knew she hadn't brought him out here to express her appreciation.

"Hey, so, I was wondering how likely it will be for me to stay on this crew."

He exhaled and looked over her shoulder. "Well, I don't know."

"Because I'd really like to stay here. I've put in my application for the hotshots twice, and I've passed the physical all three times. I've been a Captain in a rural fire department for just over a year, and I think I fit in well with the rest of the men here."

"You fit in real fine, Cora." He focused back on her again, and she appreciated the sharp glint in his eye. "We've got twenty-one on this crew right now. Me, our two captains, two squad bosses, and four senior firefighters. Those positions are all taken, and I don't see any of my men leaving for another crew or another career."

"Yeah, okay," Cora said. "So that leaves...what? Eleven other positions. Right?"

"They're mostly temp positions," Gil said. "Like what you have now."

"But Henry said he's an apprentice firefighter on the crew. What about that?" Cora's pulse pounded through her body, making her stomach sick. "And Liam said he's been a 'temp' for over a year."

Gil cocked his head and studied her. "You've done your homework."

"I want to stay on this crew, sir." She needed it as badly as she needed air. She had to have something to offer Brennan in terms of stability and a future together. "I'm a Level One Firefighter. I've taken classes in fire safety and rescue. I have two medical certifications; one's in pediatrics. I don't smoke, I don't drink, I don't gamble, and I'm about to get married." She sucked in a breath at the surety she felt about that last item.

She tried to keep the emotion out of her voice when she added, "I want to stay on this crew," but she failed. She cleared it away. "Sir."

Gil watched her, his mind clearly churning. She appreciated the way he thought, and he'd been an amazing Super out in the field. She'd learned that he'd been a hotshot for twenty years before getting this Superintendent assignment with the Del Rosa Crew, and she really wanted to work with him.

"Let me talk to my captains and see if we have room for another apprentice."

Cora sucked in a breath as her eyes widened.

"No promises," Gil said, a smile twitching at the

corners of his mouth. "And not a word of this to anyone else."

"No, sir. Not a word." Cora stood straight and tall and saluted him. "Thank you, sir."

He backed up a step and scanned her. "You're tougher than you look, Cora. I like that." He twisted the doorknob to go back inside. "No promises. And wipe that silly smile off your face before you come inside." He ducked through the doorway, and Cora spun to the forest just behind the work center. She couldn't stop smiling for a good long while, and since her phone needed to charge before she could call and tell Brennan the good news, she sank to the concrete and poured her thanks out to the Lord.

It wasn't quite warm enough for an outdoor wedding in Utah, in April. The peaks surrounding Brush Creek still had snow on them, and the trees were just starting to bud. But it was the best time for Cora to get married, and since Brennan was sick and tired of living in his lonely apartment by himself, he'd do anything to make Cora his wife.

Even wait for her at the end of an aisle in fifty-degree weather, while the wind tried to shake all the newly budded leaves free behind him.

His classes had ended the week before, and she'd been given a week of absence time from her crew for their wedding and honeymoon. It had taken months for the official paperwork to be pushed through the National Forest Service, but she'd just signed her permanent apprentice firefighter contract with the Del Rosa

Hotshot Crew. It was a good salary for them, and a dream come true for her.

She was his dream come true, and he wanted everything to be perfect for her today. So when it started raining and a general cry of dismay went up from the crowd, Brennan looked at his mother helplessly.

She stood, along with his father, and approached Brennan. "I know she wanted to be married here among the trees," she said, gesturing to the wildly waving limbs just a few feet away.

"She did." Oxbow Park was right across the street from the fire station, and it had trees like her beloved National Forests in California.

"What if we just moved over to the fire house?" his dad suggested. "If we got them to move the engines out, I bet there would be enough room to set up inside the bay."

Brennan twisted toward Station Two, wondering how much time they had before the sky opened and ruined the arch, the altar, and the balloons his sisters had set up with Helene and Laura that morning.

"Let's do it," he said, making an executive decision. Cora wouldn't see him anyway, citing the wedding tradition that it was bad luck for the groom to see his bride before she walked down the aisle.

"I'll call Laura," his mother said, and his dad started barking orders at everyone in the near vicinity.

Brennan turned to find Kent, glad his friend waited only a few paces away. "Can we get the firetrucks out of the bay? We can put the chairs in there and have some shelter from the storm."

Kent looked at Station Two and then back to Brennan, a grin spreading across his face. "Yeah, let me call Jorge and Charlie." He pulled out his phone and strode across the street while Brennan went to the nearest chairs and picked them up.

It felt like chaos, with people moving as quickly as possible in their finest dresses and best suits. But with everyone helping, it didn't take long to relocate the chairs across the street. Charlie and Kent pulled the fire engines out and into a V, creating a narrow walkway for Cora to walk through before she'd enter the now-empty bay.

The chatter sounded twice as loud indoors as it had outdoors, and Brennan adjusted his bowtie just as his mother ran into the bay and the pounding sound of rain hit the roof.

She took a moment to brush her hair back before she came to meet him near the altar. "Laura's taking care of getting Cora over here. We should be all set."

The reception would be in the little red brick church Cora had grown to love, so at least that didn't need to be re-coordinated. Brennan's nerves stretched and vibrated with every passing minute where Cora didn't walk between the two fire engines outside.

Finally, finally, Helene appeared, a teary smile on her face. She moved quickly down the aisle to sit alone—her husband still not with her. A pang of sadness pulled through Brennan when he realized she'd come alone.

Cora had been trying to get the story out of her sister for months, but Helene wouldn't tell.

But her husband's absence surely said it all, as did the way she twisted and tearfully watched as Cora's nieces and nephew started the wedding party down the aisle.

The little girls threw rose petals and blew bubbles. Her one nephew carried the ring, his head held so high, Brennan thought his neck must hurt terribly.

Then Cora appeared, her dress mushrooming out from her waist to make a five-foot circle along the ground. Brennan went completely still at the sight of her, his blood heating to lava temperatures and she hadn't even taken a step toward him yet.

Her dad came to her side and offered her his elbow. She beamed at him and pressed a quick kiss to his cheek before focusing on Brennan. They stepped forward so slowly Brennan thought he'd explode.

Finally, Chris passed Cora to Brennan, and he tucked her arm right against his side.

"Hey, you," she said, smiling at him with her gorgeous red lips and those mesmerizing eyes.

"My love." He bent down and traced his lips over her temple before facing the pastor. He'd attended three of his siblings weddings, and never had he felt this level of happiness and bliss before. He wondered if Kyler was bored, or Berlin was on her phone. He simply hadn't realized how big of an event it was to marry someone he loved. A soulmate. A forever friend.

He understood now, and as Pastor Peters began

reciting the vows they'd written for each other, Brennan couldn't help feeling a little impatient.

The click, click, click of the wedding photographer sounded in his ears, indicating that it was almost time to do what he wanted to do most: Kiss his wife.

"Do you, Cora Michelle Wesley, take this man, Brennan Cody Fuller, to be your legally and lawfully wedded husband, in sickness and in health, for better or worse, for the time you both shall live on this earth?"

"Yes," she said in a clear, loud voice that echoed off the concrete and the high ceilings.

Brennan's whole body buzzed, and when it was his turn to say "Yes," he did so in his proudest voice too.

"Then I pronounce you husband and wife." The pastor smiled and stepped back. "You may kiss your bride."

Cora giggled and traced those delicious fingernails along his neck and into his hair as he claimed her mouth with his.

"I love you," he whispered among the cheers.

"I love—"

The rest of her sentence was cut off as both fire engine sirens wailed to life, deafening Brennan and startling him away from Cora. With his heartbeat racing and adrenaline pumping through him, he found Kent behind the wheel of one engine while Charlie was laughing behind the wheel of the other.

He looked at Cora, and they burst into laughter too. Laughter which filled his soul long after the sirens had quieted and they'd been ushered down the aisle and into a waiting limousine.

With the doors closed, Brennan brushed the rain from his shoulders and looked into his wife's eyes.

"I got it all," she said, shaking her head and smiling. "I didn't think I would, but I did. I got you. I got the job. I got it all."

He kissed her and tucked her into his side. He'd gotten her, and the possibility of a new future, with a new job. "I did too," he whispered, sending a prayer of thanksgiving and gratitude heavenward for such blessings.

———

Read on for a sneak peek of the next book in the series,
THE TROOPER'S TREASURE.

Dawn Fuller couldn't stop her foot from bouncing. Her knee went up-down, up-down, up-down over and over, increasing in rate and intensity with every passing second. She kept her eyes on the ground so her hair would fall over her shoulders and hide her face.

The horrible scent of rubbing alcohol and the stringency of other medical products assaulted her, and she couldn't wait to get out of the women's clinic. Her stomach roiled, and she hoped it was all from nerves, that the test she'd just taken would be negative.

Though she was definitely living up to her label as the "wild child" of the Fuller family, she couldn't imagine walking into her conservative parent's home and telling them she was pregnant.

Only twenty-six and without a husband—or even a

boyfriend anymore—Dawn simply couldn't fathom bringing a child into the world and attempting to raise it.

Please, she prayed, though she felt like a complete loser for lifting her voice to the Lord. *Please let it be negative.* She wasn't sure what God could do now. He was all-powerful, but he couldn't un-make a baby that would've been conceived seven weeks ago.

Dawn pressed her eyes closed, her desperation surging up her throat and making her gag. How long did it take to read a pregnancy test? She'd been waiting for at least ten minutes, or so she thought. Since she'd suspected she was pregnant, every minute felt like a lifetime.

"Dawn Fuller?"

Her eyes snapped open and she stood like she'd been shot out of a cannon. "Here." She cursed herself for practically yelling like she was in school and needed to be marked present. She approached the curly-haired woman wearing pink scrubs, her feet like lead and her heart thundering in her chest.

"Here you go, sweetie." She handed her a sealed envelope and looked past Dawn like the slip of paper inside wouldn't be life-changing. Yes or no, whatever the test said, Dawn's whole life would change.

"Tara?" the nurse called, and Dawn slipped out of the women's center and back to her car. It took all her courage to slide her fingers under the flap of the envelope and rip it open. She pulled out a single third-sheet of paper that had a bunch of letters on it Dawn didn't understand.

She did, however, understand what NEGATIVE meant.

Sobs shook her shoulders, her body, and she crumpled over the steering wheel with gratitude and relief shattering through her. After the storm had blown itself out, she straightened, pushed her hair off her face, and looked out the windshield.

Drawing in a deep breath, she tried to settle herself. She needed to make the one-hour drive back to Brush Creek before she was missed.

She scoffed at herself. "No one even knows you're gone." She started the car to get the air conditioning going, and set herself north and west along the two-lane highway. She'd gone a couple of miles when her tears hit her again.

Thankfully, there wasn't anyone out here in the middle of the day, and if her car went over the center line a couple of times, it was fine. She loved driving fast in the middle of nowhere, and the soft roar of the wind as her two-seater cut through the atmosphere helped to calm her.

She glanced down at her speedometer and realized she was driving just a bit too fast, even for her. Easing up on the accelerator, she focused back out the windshield again. Movement caught her eye, and she slammed on the brakes as a deer bounded in front of her car.

Dawn screamed, yanked the wheel to the right as the

deer went left, and watched in slow motion as her car left the road and soared into the ditch.

She braced for impact, her fingers so tight against the steering wheel. The deafening sound of bending metal on scrunching metal tore through her ears. The car came to a stop and steam rose from the hood, obscuring her view.

Dawn breathed, her adrenaline so high she could barely do much more than basic bodily functions. Pain cascaded through her body, stemming from her leg. Glancing down, she found her calf stuck between the crumpled metal and the seat. Blood stained her shorts and dripped down to her shoeless foot.

Her stomach lurched. She'd never been able to stand the sight of her own blood and a whiteness covered her vision.

She tried to pull her leg out, but it was stuck. She tried to open the door, but that was stuck too. The air conditioning blew hot air now, making it hard to inhale. Panic built inside her, and she needed to get out of this car. Now.

Her fingers scrabbled for something. Something to let her out.

A moan came from her mouth, building into a scream. She pounded against the window, her gaze falling to her leg. The air left her body. She couldn't pass out here. No one knew where she was.

"Phone," she moaned, but she had no idea where her purse was. She tried the door again, to no avail.

The mania inside her faded to nothing, and she slumped against the headrest. She touched her leg, and her fingers came away sticky. Her stomach swooped, and she welcomed the unconsciousness as it swept toward her.

"Hold on!" someone yelled through the glass, and Dawn had enough energy to open her eyes and look out the window. But the gorgeous, mature face of McDermott Boyd was the last man she wanted to see.

She moaned again as the handsome State Trooper hurried around the back of the car to the passenger door. He ripped it open and peered inside. "Are you—?" He blinked, his dark eyes registering his surprise and delight. "Dawn?"

Dawn let her head flop to the opposite side. She didn't want McDermott to see her like this. Didn't want to explain anything to him. She'd grown up with the Boyd family, and though McDermott was a Brush Creek native too, it was his little brothers that were Dawn's age.

No matter what, he knew what kind of woman she was. *What kind of woman you used to be*, she told herself as he pulled her across the seat.

She screamed as white hot pain shot through her, and she looked into McDermott's panicked and concerned face before she blacked out completely.

————

THE NEXT TIME SHE WOKE, the smell of toast met her nose. Whoever had put bread in the toaster and slathered it with butter really knew her. "Mom?" She tried to push herself up and found her left leg achy, but bandaged.

"Leave her be," a man said in a soft, pleasant voice, and Dawn's eyes flew to the sliver of light coming from the doorway. "Go on, now. Go see what Nana Reba wants you to do for dinner."

The pitter of little feet sounded, and then McDermott opened the door holding a plate of toast and a glass of something she hoped was orange juice.

"Hey, you're awake." He set the food on the bedside table and switched on the lamp there. "We're at my house." He chuckled and jostled his powerful shoulders in a squirmy sort of shrug. "Well, it's my Nana Reba's house, but we live here." He sat in an armchair in the corner, near the foot of the bed. "Me and my daughter. We live here with her." He seemed to realize that he'd started rambling a bit, and he pressed his mouth into a thin line.

"What happened?" Her head ached and she touched her forehead. There were no memories there. How in the world had she gotten to McDermott Boyd's house? Why had he brought her toast? Why was her leg injured?

"You don't remember?"

She sifted through the soft thoughts in her head. "I... don't remember."

"What's the last thing you do remember?" He still wore his trooper uniform, but had discarded the hat so she could see his dark hair that he kept cropped close to his scalp.

"I, uh...." Dawn leaned back against the headboard. "I was in Vernal."

He nodded, his eyes never leaving hers. The light was too dim to read too much into his expression, but Dawn didn't like the appraising way he watched her. She felt like he was more cop in the moment than an old friend.

She didn't want to be friends with him anyway. He was a perfect gentleman, a great dad, and a widower who'd lost his wife in the worst way possible. She was a complete wreck of a human being, and she could barely look at him without a river of shame tumbling through her.

Dawn closed her eyes to block out his handsome features. "I don't remember anything after that."

"You don't know what you were doing in Vernal?" He must be able to get people to tell him anything with a honeyed voice like that.

"I can't remember."

"Well." He sighed and she imagined him stretching his long legs out in front of him. "You were driving back from something in Vernal, and a deer ran across the road. You braked to miss it, swerved, and went into the ditch."

Dawn's eyes popped open. "And you saw that?"

"I sure did. I was about a half a mile behind you and I saw you go off the road." His right eyebrow quirked. "You were driving pretty fast."

Dawn didn't remember that, but she did like to

speed in general, so she didn't contradict him. "You brought me back to your house?"

"You asked me to."

It was her turn to quirk her eyebrows, and she even added a scoff. "I don't think—"

"I pulled you out of the car, and you passed in and out of consciousness. I asked you if you needed to go to the hospital, and you begged me not to take you." He looked over to the door as it opened. "C'mon, baby. You can come in."

A blonde angel skipped into the room and went over to her father. She leaned into him, shy and forward at the same time.

McDermott looked at Dawn but didn't introduce his daughter. "She wanted to make you toast. So we'll leave you to rest and eat. I had your car towed to Mick's, so I'll drive you home whenever you want." He took his daughter's hand and led her out of the room, the doe-eyed child still silent as she went with her dad.

As soon as the door snicked closed, Dawn swung her legs over the side of the bed. The toast, once appetizing, was cold now, and she needed to get out of this room, this house, before she allowed that beautiful man to care for her.

"He already has," she muttered to herself. The thought that he'd be interested in her beyond making sure she got home safe was laughable. In any case, Dawn wasn't interested. Not anymore. She needed to get her life together before she could even think about bringing someone else into it.

But if you were ready, she thought as she stood and tested her weight on her injured leg. *Maybe you should take a closer look at McDermott.*

————

THE TROOPER'S TREASURE is available now!

The Marine's Marriage: A Fuller Family Novel - Brush Creek Cowboys Romance (Book 1): Tate Benson can't believe he's come to Nowhere, Utah, to fix up a house that hasn't been inhabited in years. But he has. Because he's retired from the Marines and looking to start a life as a police officer in small-town Brush Creek. Wren Fuller has her hands full most days running her family's company. When Tate calls and demands a maid for that morning, she decides to have the calls forwarded to her cell and go help him out. She didn't know he was moving in next door, and she's completely unprepared for his handsomeness, his kind heart, and his wounded soul. **Can Tate and Wren weather a relationship when they're also next-door neighbors?**

The Firefighter's Fiancé: A Fuller Family Novel - Brush Creek Cowboys Romance (Book 2): Cora Wesley comes to Brush Creek, hoping to get some in-the-wild firefighting training as she prepares to put in her application to be a hotshot. When she meets Brennan Fuller, the spark between them is hot and instant. As they get to know each other, her deadline is constantly looming over them, and Brennan starts to wonder if he can break ranks in the family business. He's okay mowing lawns and hanging out with his brothers, but he dreams of being able to go to college and become a landscape architect, but he's just not sure it can be done. **Will Cora and Brennan be able to endure their trials to find true love?**

The Trooper's Treasure: A Fuller Family Novel - Brush Creek Cowboys Romance (Book 3): Dawn Fuller has made some mistakes in her life, and she's not proud of the way McDermott Boyd found her off the road one day last year. She's spent a hard year wrestling with her choices and trying to fix them, glad for McDermott's acceptance and friendship. He lost his wife years ago, done his best with his daughter, and now he's ready to move on. **Can McDermott help Dawn find a way past her former mistakes and down a path that leads to love, family, and happiness?**

The Detective's Date: A Fuller Family Novel - Brush Creek Cowboys Romance (Book 4): Dahlia Reid is one of the best detectives Brush Creek and the surrounding towns has ever had. She's given up on the idea of marriage—and pleasing her mother—and has dedicated herself fully to her job. Which is great, since

one of the most perplexing cases of her career has come to town. Kyler Fuller thinks he's finally ready to move past the woman who ghosted him years ago. He's cut his hair, and he's ready to start dating. Too bad every woman he's been out with is about as interesting as a lamppost—until Dahlia. He finds her beautiful, her quick wit a breath of fresh air, and her intelligence sexy. **Can Kyler and Dahlia use their faith to find a way through the obstacles threatening to keep them apart?**

The Paramedic's Partner: A Fuller Family Novel - Brush Creek Cowboys Romance (Book 5): Jazzy Fuller has always been overshadowed by her prettier, more popular twin, Fabiana. Fabi meets paramedic Max Robinson at the park and sets a date with him only to come down with the flu. So she convinces Jazzy to cut her hair and take her place on the date. And the spark between Jazzy and Max is hot and instant...if only he knew she wasn't her sister, Fabi.

Max drives the ambulance for the town of Brush Creek with is partner Ed Moon, and neither of them have been all that lucky in love. Until Max suggests to who he thinks is Fabi that they should double with Ed and Jazzy. They do, and Fabi is smitten with the steady, strong Ed Moon. **As each twin falls further and further in love with their respective paramedic, it becomes obvious they'll need to come clean about the switcheroo sooner rather than later...or risk losing their hearts.**

The Chief's Catch: A Fuller Family Novel - Brush Creek Cowboys Romance (Book 6): Berlin Fuller has struck out with the dating scene in Brush Creek more times than she cares to admit. When she makes a deal with her friends that they can choose the next man she goes out with, she didn't dream they'd pick surly

Cole Fairbanks, the new Chief of Police.

His friends call him the Beast and challenge him to complete ten dates that summer or give up his bonus check. When Berlin approaches him, stuttering about the deal with her friends and claiming they don't actually have to go out, he's intrigued. As the summer passes, Cole finds himself burning both ends of the candle to keep up with his job and his new relationship. **When he unleashes the Beast one time too many, Berlin will have to decide if she can tame him or if she should walk away.**

IVORY PEAKS FARM
ROMANCE SERIES

Experience true Rocky Mountain life in the Ivory Peaks Romance series! You'll get more Hammond family romance, second chance romance, and all the heartwarming and uplifting family fiction you're craving. Ivory Peaks is the perfect escape for anyone looking to feel loved, cherished, and like they belong. You belong right here in Ivory Peaks!

His First Love (Book 1): She broke up with him a decade ago. He's back in town after finishing a degree at MIT, ready to start his job at the family company. Can Hunter and Molly find their way through their pasts to build a future together? Can his first love be the one that becomes forever?

Go up the canyon to Brush Creek Ranch, where a community of retired rodeo cowboys are looking for love...

Brush Creek Cowboy (Book 1): He's a cowboy raising his son alone. She's a widow with a chocolate obsession. **Can Brush Creek cowboy Walker get over his losses and fears in order to build a future with Tess?**

Coral Canyon Cowboys Romance Series

Visit stunning Wyoming for another family of cowboys... The Youngs! The series includes second chance romance, friends to lovers, family saga, Christian values, clean and sweet romance, single dads, equine therapy themes, police dog training, brotherly relationships, return to hometown, fish out of water, and country music stars!

Tex (Book 1): He's back in town after a successful country music career. She owns a bordering farm to the family land he wants to buy...and she outbids him at the auction. **Can Tex and Abigail rekindle their old flame, or will the issue of land ownership come between them?**

About Liz

Liz Isaacson writes inspirational romance, usually set in Texas, or Wyoming, or anywhere else horses and cowboys exist. She lives in Utah, where she writes full-time, takes her two dogs to the park everyday, and eats a lot of veggies while writing. Find her on her website, along with all of her pen names, at feelgoodfictionbooks.com.

www.ingramcontent.com/pod-product-compliance
Lightning Source LLC
Chambersburg PA
CBHW031331060726
47590CB00007B/2428

9781638760887